Mary Atkins

Little Pea-Nut Merchant, or, Harvard's Aspirations

Mary Atkins

Little Pea-Nut Merchant, or, Harvard's Aspirations

ISBN/EAN: 9783337196776

Printed in Europe, USA, Canada, Australia, Japan

Cover: Foto ©Andreas Hilbeck / pixelio.de

More available books at **www.hansebooks.com**

LITTLE

OR,

HARVARD'S ASPIRATIONS.

BOSTON:
HENRY A. YOUNG & CO.,
No. 24 CORNHILL.

CONTENTS.

3

CHAPTER VIII.

CHAPTER IX.

CHAPTER X.

CHAPTER XI.

CHAPTER XII.

CHAPTER XIII.

CHAPTER XIV.

CHAPTER XV.

THE LITTLE PEA-NUT MERCHANT.

———∞⚬∞———

CHAPTER I.

BAD TIDINGS.

" Though He slay me, yet will I trust in Him."

ANY letter for me to-day, Abel?" asked
Dariel Leighton, in an eager, excited
tone, as he jumped from the hedge where
he had been waiting a full hour, and suddenly
arrested the lymphatic penny-post, who groaned
along as if toiling beneath a summer sky, and
much more heavily burdened than he was, for
his package of letters was scarcely larger than
a child's primer.

But it was not a summer sky that bent blue
and broad over the twain. Nor were the

thoughts of one, at least, of these widely different men, fresh, joyous, and glowing like summer. Far from it. The year had fallen into
the sere and yellow leaf, as every inch of the
landscape declared. So, also, had Dariel, as
his seamed countenance abundantly testified.
Yet his spirit was usually like that of youth,
hopeful, elastic, overflowing with faith and
pleasant anticipations. Abel looked up at the
questioner, and, with a snort, expressive of dis-
gust at anything like haste or excitement, lazily drew forth a red cotton handkerchief, and,
slowly drawing it across his rubicund face, occupied the next minute or two to his own satisfaction, if not to his companion's. After placing this part of his wardrobe where it belonged,
he honored poor Dariel with another dissatisfied snort, then good-naturedly replied, —

"Don't know — I'll look. May be there
may be, and may be there mayn't. No telling

which till a body's looked. I suppose you'll
'low me time to look ? "

" Do hurry !" answered Dariel, restive under such unnecessary delay.

" You're narvous, and all up in a flutter
I never flutter, — it stirs up a man's narves
to flutter," expostulated Abel, loitering and
panting as only the lymphatic can.

" I dare say you are never nervous, Abel.
I am glad you are not. Ready to look now,
my good fellow ?" coaxingly said Dariel,
aware that he had made a mistake in trying to
hurry the other.

" Yes, I'll look," came in answer, when the
package had been unloosed from its elastic
band.

Dariel drew close to Abel, and looked over
his shoulder to read the superscription of every
letter until his should turn up. But there was
none for him. This fact was expressed by a
sigh, as he drew off, and hastily dashed his

horny hand across his eyes, where tears had forced themselves.

" Too bad ! " said Abel, in a tone of sympathy, seating himself on the hedge, inly overjoyed at an opportunity to rest and gossip.

" I hardly dared hope there would be a letter for me," almost sobbed Dariel.

" Now, my old friend, don't be so downhearted, for your turn 'll come next, see if it don't, or time after ? Everybody's turn comes sometime, I always notice," philosophized Abel from his perch, lazily throwing acorns at a lame toad hobbling towards some place secure from such assaults.

" Certainly. Providence don't pour out his blessings all in one line, I ought to know," said Dariel, reverently lifting his hat, and raising his eyes heavenward, yet, in spite of himself, with the slightest tinge of sadness in his tone, as he added, —

" I'll be waiting here when you take your

afternoon tramp. *Perhaps* then you'll have the letter I want."

" Maybe," responded Abel.

" I hope there'll be good news for me soon, I'm sure."

" It's a fall in stocks that troubles you, or something of that sort, I reckon?"

" Bad investments, Abel. I had but a trifle to put that way," replied Dariel, humbly, but adding angrily, " a little is too much for *me* to lose, you know."

" True enough. Now I have nothing to do with such matters. Wife sees to all the surplus money. It's in her to manage, and I let her, for my business is enough for me to do. Carrying about letters that an't for one's self, and to people that are allus in a hurry to get 'em, isn't the easiest business in the world."

Here Abel paused to breathe, and further express, by an upward turn of his small eyes, how laborious was the business he daily followed.

"As I said before," observed Dariel, "I'll be waiting here this afternoon." And he moved homeward.

"Stop! What's yer hurry? I thought we were going to have a nice talk," shouted Abel.

"But the letters, friend, — you forget those," replied Dariel, still moving off.

"A few minutes either way don't make much difference, I reckon," muttered Abel, settling himself farther into the hedge, and persecuting the lame toad afresh, as it thrust its head from under a plantain-leaf to reconnoiter the whereabouts of his enemy.

But, wait and hope to his utmost, old Dariel received no letter that afternoon, nor for a week afterwards. When it came, it only made him the more sad in face and manner, for it brought him bad tidings. He had opened it, and while Abel, from the fullness of sympathy, looked over his shoulder upon the blighting page, read it aloud with tearful eyes. Then he folded up the letter, and without another word went home. **For once,** Abel hurried his letters to their owners. **Then he** hurried himself home, in order to communicate to his wife the ill-tidings Dariel had received.

Mrs. Lumbkin, who, in the midst of a week's mending, happened to look out at the window in front of which she sat, beheld her husband thus hurrying, and, **full** of fears and surmises, went to the gate to meet him.

"**What is the** matter, Abel ? **Don't** hurry so ; you aren't used to it ! " she cried.

"Never worry about *me,* **Dolly.** I've got bad news for you," panted Abel.

" Has anything happened **to** our boy ?" cried **Mrs.** Lumbkin, grasping her husband's arm.

" Not a thing ; Bob is safe. The bad news don't touch us, only as we feel for an upright old man in trouble, Dolly ! "

" Oh," sighed Mrs. Lumbkir, greatly relieved. "But come and rest yourself before you speak another word. Such a heat as you are in!" And Mrs. Lumbkin led her husband into the house, passed him a chair, and, fanning him, again bade him speak not a word until he had rested. Yet, devoted wife that she was, she longed for the tidings that had so strangely moved her not easily-shaken husband. At last Abel said, —

"If you're willing, — I mean if you think I'm rested, — I'll tell you the story now."

"Your face is looking natural once more, so you may," replied Mrs. Lumbkin.

"Well, then, Dariel Leighton is a poor man. All that he had, was in stocks that are flat enough in the dust now."

"And at his age, too! But he'll never want for bread; nobody ever knew him to be a Dives in spirit, husband!"

"Just so, Dolly. You allus hit the truth."

" Do you know what he means to do for a living ? "

" No, wife ; for he couldn't talk much after he'd read his letter. He was all down, like."

" But he'll not be down long. He can't be, for he has that which'll keep him up," gravely responded Mrs. Lumbkin.

Abel dropped his eyes, conscious that *he* was deficient in that which would lift his aged friend above the gloom of the present.

" Has Dariel much, in the way of food and fuel, laid in for winter ? "

" Little enough I reckon, wife."

" Then we can send him potatoes and pork, husband, if you are willing." And Mrs. Lumbkin's pleasant face looked all the pleasanter for the suggestion.

" Ay, that we can, wife, and thank ye for mentioning it. Have ye anything else to give him ? "

" Yes, there's a web of shirting, yet whole.

Now I might work some of that up for him, and you not miss it ever.   May I?"

" You may do whatever you like, and I can never think it wrong; 'cos why? 'Cos the wrong isn't in ye, Dolly."

" Oh, Abel, there's a heap of wrong in me."

" I can't see any ; and never could, wife."

" But there is, husband," gravely persisted Mrs. Lumbkin, with a yearning look in her face that Abel could not well stand.

Whatever it was she possessed unshared by him, he reverenced her for it, and meant " some day to set about getting it for himself."

Thus divided in spirit stand many a husband and wife, and with much sorrow and deep wrestling in prayer to the one whose calling and election is sure through our Lord Jesus Christ.

That evening, Mr. and Mrs. Lumbkin made Dariel a visit.   They found him sitting in the porch, an open Bible upon his knee.   With a smile he welcomed them, and, when Mrs. Lumbkin said, " How fortunate that you know where to find comfort!" replied fervently, as he grasped her outstretched hand,—

" Yes, that is my joy! God never leaves us comfortless. How boundless is his goodness!"

Abel walked to the window, and looked with rather misty eyes upon the fading landscape.

" It is *boundless goodness* that takes such care of us erring creatures every day."

"I know it, Mrs. Lumbkin, and that is why I can not feel the loss of my little property as much as I should have felt it years ago, before I knew the wealth He gives us in His blessed word. Although I have only this poor roof above my head, yet somehow I feel rich as a king to-night, my friends."

"And you have more wealth than most kings," replied Mrs. Lumbkin, in a voice that set her husband's eyes in a great mist again

"Some day I must set about finding this wealth," mentally soliloquized Abel, his broad and well-clothed back to the others. Not willing to listen longer to the conversation, he told Dariel that he had a deal more pork and potatoes than he could use, and would be glad if his old friend would accept it. Mrs. Lumbkin did not mention the shirts she proposed to make and present, as Dariel seemed fully enough overcome with what Abel had promised.

Dariel was a bachelor, and lived alone in a bit of a two-room cottage close to the sea, whose tirelesss throbbings made the sweetest of music for him, for all through the early and middle part of his life he had followed and honored the occupation of sailor. He had been prudent, but never mean nor uncharitable, and his little savings had been carefully invested against that time when trembling hands, tottering footsteps, and failing faculties, show that the strong man is strong no longer. But, as we have seen, his wealth had gone to the winds, and Dariel Leighton, already three-score years, was poor.

2

CHAPTER II.

"The rich and the poor meet together ; the Lord is the Maker of them all."

AUTUMN had given place to winter, and one day, when the sun was shining gorgeously upon icicled trees and white-robed streets and lanes, a sleigh whirled up to Dariel's humble door, and out jumped a fine-looking lad of fourteen years, who rapped loudly with the butt end of his whip to announce his approach. Dariel hastened to open the door.

" Ah, Dariel, how are you ? " shouted the lad, taking between his own fair, handsome hands the hard, wrinkled ones of the other.

" Of all whom I would most like to see you are the one, Master Hoyt! When did you come home ? Come in, my lad. You know not how

18

I have longed to see you in my house once more!"

"You have really, Dariel!"

"Ay, that I have. You are in good health, I can tell by your ruddy cheek."

"Capital! But you are not, I fear. Is it true that you have lost your earnings?"

"Yes; all but this home."

"And this a mere rat-trap! Excuse me, Dariel. But it never struck me as half good and large enough for you. But why did you not let me know of your misfortune? It has worn upon your looks."

"I don't like to cloud the brow of youth unnecessarily."

"Nor lighten, when *necessary*, heavy pockets, it seems. But as long as Warren Hoyt has a dime, he will share it with honest **Dariel Leighton**!"

Thus merrily speaking, Warren made a humorous dash at his pocket, from whence he drew up a purse, at each end of which hung a small heap of valuable bills.

"You observe, Dariel, I have just received my quarterly allowance. All the better for you! I mean to share it even. Now protest against it, will you, and thus hinder an idle lad from performing one good deed."

"But I don't need so much. It would be selfish in me to accept it," pleaded Dariel, looking perplexedly upon two ten-dollar bills.

"If you refuse it, you'll offend me. If I keep it, I shall spend it on trifles: cigars, very likely."

"Do you smoke?" gravely inquired Dariel, while a troubled look overspread his face.

"'Like a soger!' Why not? All the boys at school do; on the sly, of course."

"It is a bad habit, and too often leads to other bad habits, my child. Besides, it is a sin to deceive your teachers."

"Ah! now you think I need a sermon. Well,

preach away. I shall not easily tire of your preaching, which I know is unselfish and sincere, Dariel."

"But I wish you would drop the habit."

"Maybe I will, some time. At any rate, your advice is worth taking. And so your little property has vanished, Mrs. Lumbkin told me. I called there on my way here; oh, and, by the way, she gave me a bundle to bring you. I found her baking gingerbread, and, learning my intention to call here, she gave me a huge pan for you, after treating me bountifully." And Warren rushed to his sleigh, from the box of which he produced a brown paper parcel, which he placed in Dariel's hand.

"She and Abel have been good friends to me."

"I dare say," replied Warren, sobering both face and voice to add, "I always found them true and kind enough. Mrs. Lumbkin says I grow more like my mother every day. Do you think so, Dariel?"

"Yes, Master Warren ; yet you are a Hoyt."

"Then I resemble both parents : I like that. All the other boys have some relatives to welcome them home, but," with a sigh, "I have none. It is a sad thing to be an orphan, Dariel. I often set myself to wondering what my parents were like, and how they looked." And Warren sighed again, and tried to hide a tear. But Dariel, who had well known and clearly remembered these lamented parents, covered his face with his handkerchief, and sobbed, which had the effect of causing Warren's eyes to fill and overflow, much against his efforts to be manly, for he had a boy's idea that weeping was effeminate.

"Were my mother's voice and manners sweet, Dariel?"

Warren had often asked the question before,

for his curiosity regarding his parents was insatiate.

" Sweet as both could be. She was as refined and gentle-hearted a lady as one is likely to see."

" And all about her loved her ? "

" That they did, my lad."

" And my father, — was he as good as my mother ? " He spoke in a lower tone now.

" He was a large-hearted man, and pleasant-voiced," restrainedly answered Dariel, feeling uneasy.

" But was he my mother's match in goodness ? " persisted Warren, with the unquenchable curiosity that had ever tormented him about his father, of whom few were willing to speak to him.

" Few husbands are equal to their wives, as far as I have noticed," replied Dariel, who, through his own mother, revered the sex, and who, strongly desirous of turning the conversation, began to speak of other matters.

Warren, after a long-drawn sigh, and quickly suppressed pain at his heart, fell in with Dariel's talk; but it was plain to be seen that the spring had departed from his spirit.

Dariel could not permit his youthful visitor to leave until he had given him good advice, which was gravely listened to. Somehow Warren could not help associating this advice with the parent of whom Dariel was so unwilling to speak at length.

"Above all," said Dariel in conclusion, "remember to pray often to your heavenly Father. Prayer is a great safeguard, young master. It has carried me through great straits. When I lost my little property, I felt like one tried beyond his deserts, and wondered for a short time what good I had got by striving to do my duty to God and man. Happily, I remembered that more of good than ill had followed me through all my length of days. And ought I to murmur when now, just as I had so nearly finished my time, a little heavier shadow has been permitted to settle upon me? Of course not! And as it was with me, so it is with all, if we will only see it, — more of good than ill is given us. And that it is so is a wonderful mercy, when we think how wicked we are by nature, and how we keep sinning, and how ungrateful and indifferent we are to the Giver of all things."

"And so that all means that I am to look on the bright side, and not stop to mourn, if I am troubled and an orphan," sighed Warren.

"Yes; for God has given you many blessings, and out of those blessings you can set little or great streams of mercy running hither and thither, all about, every one of them to bring back rich returns to your own soul."

"I can do good with my wealth; and you will show me how, Dariel!" replied Warren, quite animated, the brightness of his morning sun shining out the clearer for the darkening we have witnessed.

" I will help you all I can, but your own generous spirit will soon outrun all need of me, more especially if it be bathed in celestial waters; for oh, my son, you must be a Christian, and now ! "

Then Dariel, in his earnestness, dropped upon his knees, and, drawing Warren down beside him, prayed that God's grace might be poured abundantly upon the orphan boy, who, touched and tearful, soon after took his leave.

Dariel felt well and strong enough to do something for himself. His spirit chafed at the idea of dependence. Although grateful for the generous gifts of many friends, he resolved to maintain himself. To this end he applied himself to the proper construction of an advertisement. He was a well-informed man, and particularly competent to teach navigation, and was desirous of forming a class in that science. As soon as Abel Lumbkin saw the advertisement, he hurried to Dariel, and said, —

" If you'll have some circulars struck off, I'll leave them at houses where I take my letters Everybody don't take the newspaper, and, because everybody don't, it mayn't be known everywhere that you want to teach navigation. I reckon you won't object to having a sight of scholars if you can get them, old friend ? "

" Far from it. I would like a large class. How good in you to think of circulars for me ! " replied Dariel, much moved.

" It wasn't me ; it was Dolly," said Abel, with a glow of satisfaction and pride.

" An estimable woman is she, full of good, unselfish thoughts," returned Dariel, warmly

Abel's round face was suffused with smiles, for he liked to hear his wife praised ; and his taking about the circulars proved a good thing

for Dariel, who all through the winter had
scholars in plenty. And this labor, which he
found very pleasant, brought him in money
enough, not only for his own wants, but to
drop into the missionary-box, and to help the
poor about him. Thus one whose heart has
been renewed by grace, and whose nature is
improved thereby, is always seeing openings
through which the hand of mercy is beckon-
ing to new works. Among Dariel's pupils was
one young man whose conversation was inter-
larded with oaths. This the veteran could not
stand. Most faithfully he set himself to turn
the profane tongue to utter words of praise.
In after years this pupil became a wealthy and
generous merchant, whose Christian life was a
lesson and a blessing. Others of the class
also turned, with heavenly rejoicings, from the
evil of their ways. And thus, ere he was
scarcely aware, Dariel became the bearer of
many glad t'dings, not the least of which was,

" They that seek me early shall find me."
" God so loved the world that he gave his only-
begotten Son, that whosoever believeth in Him
should not perish, but have everlasting life."
" This is a faithful saying, and worthy of all
acceptation, that Christ Jesus came into the
world to save sinners." " The blood of Jesus Christ his Son cleanseth from all sin."
" Who his own self bare our sins in his own
body on the tree."

And so it happened that while these pupils
were learning paths over the trackless seas,
they were also learning the way to the
throne of the great Maker of those seas.

One evening, when the class had ended their
lessons, the pupil whose profanity had so
shocked Dariel made a proposition, which met
with general favor. It was this:

" Boys, as we are so soon to separate, let us
promise that wherever we are, henceforward
we will open and close the first day of every

month with a prayer for each other. Let it be
a mutual prayer-time, to be sacredly kept up
as long as we live. And in our prayers let us
never fail to remember, as long as he lives,
one whose watchful care placed us Zionward;
surely, we were sent here by Providence to be
taught it."

Dariel's tears fell upon his cheeks while
these words were being uttered. All the pupils assented to this proposition, and, gathering
about their aged teacher, who had fallen upon
his knees, they gently laid their hands upon
his hoary head, while he commended them to
the guardianship of the Father.

When spring had gayly painted hill and dell,
and scattered perfumes on the breeze, and sent
floating all about hosts of tiny songsters, every
member of Dariel's first class was being borne
to foreign climes. But, though truly loved and
sadly missed, Dariel was resigned to their loss,
being sure of their affection; and, trusting to

meet them again, he spent no time in useless repinings. A new class, good spirits, and tolerable health, made spring and summer fly by on pleasant wings.

Meanwhile the Lumbkin family prospered; and, if slowly, Abel was learning great and last ing truths appertaining to his eternal good.

For a while we will leave these friends, and learn something of Warren **Hoyt,** — father of our hero.

CHAPTER III.

> " A world where lust of pleasure, grandeur, gold, —
> Three demons that divide its realms between them, —
> With strokes alternate buffet to and fro
> Man's restless heart, their sport, their flying ball."

THE savings of two griping grandfathers formed themselves into a " silver spoon " for Warren Hoyt, on his advent upon this stage of existence. In admiration of which shining gift, many beholders lost sight of the endless poverty the same hour gave him in gently stilling for ever the heart of the fair young mother, — a poverty, alas! that the orphan can never realize the extent of. The infant's father had gone before; hence its capacities were unfolded by those whose care and sympathy were measured by the value of their golden rewards. He soon perceived this, and

32

oftèn, when noticing the parental guardianship enjoyed by his playmates, wished, with bitterness that he could not easily repress, — for
he was a child of deep feelings, — that the same
affectionate care had been permitted to bless
and shelter him. But these feelings he seldom
made apparent, for he soon found it to be of
no use, as he met little besides surprise, du-
plicity, indifference, or misconstruction in return ; and he grew too proud to complain to
or confide in those whose entire services showed
them to be indeed his inferiors. But these rev-
elations, coming as they did through experience,
gave him thorough contempt for gold, and as
irrepressible longings for the time when he
could dismiss his selfish hirelings and his indifferent guardian, and gather about him something that would love him for himself alone.
He had not a clear idea what that something
would be, and he wept stealthy tears when he
reflected it could not be parents, — a father

and mother, — treasures that often in dreams blessed with gentle ministrations his slumbers.

But this indefinite void **formed itself into a joyful** reality when the **good,** kind face of Dariel Leighton beamed upon him in his solitude. And this happened six years before, when Dariel gave up the seas and resolved to "settle down" for life. He had made his first voyage under the captaincy of Warren's maternal grandfather, a man who, if close, never forgot honest, unassuming worth. One day, **when** Dariel was walking meditatively **along** the beach, he beheld a little child quite too near the inrolling waves. Its nurse was chatting with other idle, thoughtless young women, unmindful **of the danger of her** charge. But Dariel sternly recalled her to her duty, and in so doing arrested the attention of the child, whose sad eyes lighted up with gratitude as he cried, —

"I was getting afraid of the water, it came

so near, and **nobody to keep** it off. I was so dizzy."

" How came he to know I was nurse to Warren ? " mumbled the nurse, twitching **at the** child's sleeve, to draw him away from Dariel.

" The child in his fright called ' Nancy ! ' **so did** your companions in your idle chatting. I knew you to be his nurse **by** that," pleasantly replied Dariel, keeping **the** child a little to ask **its name.**

" Warren Hoyt," was the answer, and the speaker threw his arms about Dariel's neck, and lavished kisses on the weather-beaten cheek.

All this innocent joy was **not lost** upon **Dariel,** who resolved **to see** the child often. Besides, the respect he had always paid the grandfather (long since deceased) was easily and naturally transferred to the grandchild, whose winning ways, and unselfish affection soon drew forth a far warmer sentiment than respect.

With childish frankness and unstudied elo-

quence, Warren soon told Dariel how lonely he
had been. Nor did Dariel think this disclosure
strange, but listened sweetly to it; for, from
the first glimpse of the child so near a watery
grave, he saw the shadow that death had cast
upon the wings of that young life, in their first
faint flutterings. The friendship so pleasantly
commenced had continued without intermission
for four years, when it was thought advisable
to send Warren away to school. The boy wept
bitter tears at parting with Dariel, whose grief
was equal; but both were comforted by thoughts
of frequent letters, and the long yearly vaca-
tion.

Warren reached his fourteenth year, but the
birthday was passed at school, and unnoticed
by any one but Dariel and Mrs. Lumbkin, the
former of whom contributed a long, newsy letter, containing many expressions of interest
and affection, and the latter a box of " goodies."
But deep in the pleasure of the first, and shar-

ing the last with his chums, the lonely boy was far from unhappy on his birthday. He possessed great beauty of person and address; flexibility of character; warm, quick sympathies, and a loving heart. He was considered a good scholar, the best in his class, for he liked study, and, besides, labored to win the approbation of his teachers. But he was regarded quite unfavorably by one of his schoolmates, who possessed an envious and jealous disposition. This lad's name was Torrey. His home was in Borden, a large city, and the scene of our story, where also our other characters resided. He was in the habit of occasionally throwing out unpleasant hints touching Warren's father, and exulted in the misery this cruelty occasioned. The orphan at such times, hiding his emotion as best he might, always resolved to question Dariel, but, as we have seen, with little success. At eighteen Warren entered college, where he still ranked above Eben Torrey.

In these four years, Dariel had been very comfortable by means of teaching, but he was growing more feeble, although his mind was still unimpaired. Enduring lessons from the fountain of celestial knowledge did he strive to impart, and for this grew more into the love of his charge. One morning, while Dariel sat beneath a tree in his garden, surrounded by his pupils, Abel brought him a letter.

"It is from Warren," said Dariel, glancing at the superscription.

"As Dolly 'll want to hear from him, s'pose I stop while you read it," said Abel, seating himself upon the grass, and smiling benignly upon the scholars.

"He writes that he has graduated in a manner of which he need not feel ashamed, and is going to Niagara with the Mayburns. He will be absent a month, after which he will return, and put Auburndale in fine trim. He sends his love to Mrs. Lumbkin and you," said Dariel, when he had read the letter through.

"The Mayburns of Willowglen, most likely. Their place is famous for its willows," said Abel, pondering the matter over.

In six weeks from that time Warren returned to Borden, and hurried to his old friend. Never had he looked so attractive to Dariel's eyes.

After he had talked awhile upon indifferent matters and in an abstracted manner, he blushed, stammered, and finally informed Dariel that he was about to marry.

"Marry,—*you* marry! My son, that is a great step for a man to take," with difficulty replied Dariel, growing pale from surprise.

"I know it. But I can't live in my great house all alone," stammered Warren, rather hurt by Dariel's manner. He continued, "I am a lonely being. Nobody but Marion would care a cent for me if I had not wealth, with the exception of yourself and Dolly Lumbkin. I have never known what *home* is. I wish and mean to." And ere he closed, the young man's face beamed with sweet anticipations, all springing from new sources of happiness. Dariel dropped his eyes to gaze on the memory of just such a scene twenty-three years ago. There must have been something there of anguish and sorrow, for tears rushed to the old man's eyes, while a dull pain throbbed at his heart. Warren noticed how pallid had grown the wrinkled cheek, and bit his lips with vexation. At last Dariel spoke again.

" My son, as never before does my old heart thrill with love for you. I have watched your career with pride from the first moment of my meeting you. In all but one thing have you satisfied the yearnings of my old heart." And here Dariel paused to gather strength, for he

was terribly shaken. At last he solemnly
added, —

" ' One thing thou lackest ! ' Without it, the
world, of which you have seen little, will, I
fear, prove too much for you."

" Oh, Dariel, I know the hidden meaning of
all this ! " cried Warren. " You are anxious
to spare my feelings, yet you wish to put me
on my guard. Eben Torrey was less careful of
wounding me. Many an hour of agony did he
cause me." And the young man rose and
paced the floor, while his clenched fists and
flashing eye told of no pleasant frame of mind.
At length calming himself, he again took a seat
beside his old friend, who was deeply overcome,
and who seemed to have lost all power of speech.
" My poor father was no Christian ? " was whis-
peringly asked by Warren, who dreaded to hear
the answer.

" Not in health. But beside the death-bed
the Saviour stood to fill the broken spirit with

heavenly love, and bear it sweetly to the Father. **My son, I could not wish for you** a more lovely death-bed. **All** of the bitterness **of** temporal partings was **lost in the** glimpses **of** celestial glory granted to the closing life. Even your mother's heart was comforted, for she saw on the face of the dying such a light as she had never seen there before. It was as if a finger from the Jordan side had touched with heavenly brightness the ashen face, to transfigure it with a beauty that earth wots not of. **And** when the last sigh was wafted, and when by that signal we knew the beautiful form was empty of **the** vital spark, your mother in tones of rapture murmured, ' Even so, Father ! ' And then her faithful nurse, Mrs. Lumbkin, all full of tears and feeling, whispered to me, ' **She** knows she will follow him soon.' And she did."

During this recital, Warren had been quietly weeping. After a pause, Dariel resumed : -- " But far better in all things is it to make life, early life, sacred to good works through the pardoning love of Christ, than to put **off** accepting it until the eleventh hour. All are not able at that time to reach forth for it. O, my son, put not off your salvation until the eleventh hour! Seek it now, and your life will be **the nobler,** your aim the higher, your affections **the** purer, for it. Without it you have no safeguard, you are liable to be tempted, and may **fall.**" Here Dariel abruptly paused.

Warren left soon after, and, riding home alone, he thought, as he lifted his eye to the starlight sky, so radiant with proof of God's power and kindness, how good a thing it must be to consecrate one's life to the praise and service of Christ. But his next morning's visit **to** Miss Mayburn dispelled such reflections, for she was gay and fashionable, and came of a gay and fashionable family.

The wealth of Warren pleased Mr. Mayburn,

while the new-born joy of Marion chimed with a purer sentiment in the maternal heart.

One evening Lina, the little sister of Marion, caught some words from her attendant, Nurse Collins, that were troublesome. She could not make their meaning out, and so resolved to ask nurse, who answered uneasily, —

"You must not mind my mutterings. Old people often talk to themselves, you know."

"Yes; but the words were queer. You said, ' What if my dear young lady were to marry a *drunkard?'* Now, nurse, you looked so sorry that you must mean Marion. Nurse, what is a drunkard ? "

"Hush! I can not tell you. You are too young to think of such matters." But nurse was weeping, and that fact did not tend to dispel Lina's curiosity. Nurse was getting garrulous, and added to this was such a desire to indulge her pet that, despite prudence and propriety, she soon launched into the affecting story of her own life.

" A drunkard is one who gives up everything for the love of wine, brandy, or any intoxicating drink ; and in consequence brings upon his family such trials as only the family of a drunkard can experience."

" Oh, nurse, can you know what these trials mean ? "

" As only few women, wives, mothers do ! "

And now Lina, who is a child of quick, delicate sympathies, is weeping convulsively in nurse's arms, which are thrown protectingly around her. Such sweet, genuine sympathy, in connection with her interest in the giver, unlocked the secret of wrongs that lived in the memory of Nurse Collins as though written with a pen of fire. With much effort she continued her story.

" When I was married, I thought myself the most fortunate woman in the world. My husband's kindness, devotedness, prudence, and industry furnished for me a comfortable home. My affairs went on smoothly until after my Margaret was born ; then my husband *tasted his first glass.*" A flood of tears for a while prevented the continuance of the story. When able, nurse resumed, " Oh, the horror of that glass! Surely some demon lurked in the bottom of it, some demon that envied me my happiness, and did not rest until it was swallowed up in misery. Margaret was my third child. I tried to make her lot easy, for, poor child, I knew how soon she would be driven forth to labor. Before she was eight years old her two elder sisters had died from exposure to all sorts of weather, and hard work in the mill. What my feelings were when kneeling over their graves, One only can tell. Their father might just as well have murdered them outright as have driven them to their end in the way he did. I taught Margaret and Eddie, my youngest, both to hate, abhor intoxicating drink. Mothers have this chance, thank God! Ah, Lina, never marry any but a strictly temperance man. You can not count upon long-continued happiness unless you do. My husband was a temperance man when I married him; his first **glass was his ruin.**"

"Then **how** could **I** be safe, any way, nurse?"

" By choosing one who has, deeper than anything else in his heart, the love and fear of God. This my poor husband lacked. I should have bidden you never marry any but a truly *Christian* man,—that would have taken in my whole meaning. **My** husband was temperate not through principle, but because he had not happened to be in the way of drinking influences. Ah, my little son, how can I again take up your **story?** He was a delicate child, feeble from his birth. One day my poor husband left his work, and came home to prepare to go into the woods gunning. His step was unsteady, his eye wavering, his manner jocosely reckless. I begged him to stay at home. He well knew why.

" ' Nay, wife ; ·I shall go, and Eddie shall go too,' he declared. Eddie clapped his hands with delight. He had never looked in better health and spirits. And how pretty he was! I clasped him in my arms, as I said piteously, ' Won't you wait until I can go with you, Eddie? Perhaps the next time father is ready to go, we can all go with him.' Margaret was sick at the time. Eddie looked wishfully up at me. The temptation to go was very strong. Yet that he wished to obey me, I clearly saw. ' He's going to-day, dame,' broke in my husband, as he bore my precious boy from the house. Not an hour had passed ere Eddie came back to me ; but how? He was *dead.* His father had accidentally shot him. When my poor husband realized what he had done, he drowned himself. This, Lina, all came from that *first glass.* When I recovered from the illness into which I was thrown by these distressing circumstances, I took Margaret and came to Borden, where, in this blessed house, I have lived ever since."

With the end of her sorrowful story, nurse, who had striven to maintain composure, rocked wildly to and fro, clasping Lina in her arms, and sobbing as if her heart would break.

" Lina, little pet, where are you ? " was heard from the foot of the grand staircase.

" My ! there's mistress' voice, and you not dressed, and the company arrived ! I must go to the door, or she'll be up here."

" Nurse, tell mamma, please, I'll hurry down," said Lina, who had not intended to go, for she did not like going into company.

Nurse went to the door, and repeated Lina's words.

" Have you taken cold, nurse ? Your voice

4

has a husky sound," said Mrs. Mayburn, kindly. "No, ma'am; thank you," replied nurse. Nurse returned to the chamber, saying, —

"Now, Lina, I'm ready to dress you like a queen." But the prospective queen could not assist nurse in her decorative attempts. She had fainted.

"My story was too much for her nerves. I might have known it. Below stairs must not hear of this," said nurse.

And nurse's efforts at resuscitation were successful. In a half hour Lina was herself.

"I am all well now, nurse. Please to dress me. I would not fail to go down now for anything," she said. Her manner had something inexpressibly touching in it as she went below, and approached and kept near Warren.

When the house was quiet, and Marion had been in her room a while, the door was carefully opened, and a little figure with curls of gold streaming over her long white dress crept cau-

tiously across the floor until it reached the bed,
where it paused as if with uncertainty.

" Lina ? "

" It is I. But I didn't know you were awake,
you were lying so still. I was afraid to wake
you."

" Have you come to sleep with me ? "

" Yes, sister Marion."

" There's a darling ! But what a pale, grave
one it is ! You look as if you ' could a tale un-
fold, whose lightest word would harrow up — ' "

" Oh, stop, Marion ! "

" What does ail the child ? Here, let me
draw you into bed. You look like a spirit,
standing there so pale and still ! "

And Marion, with a funny grimace, drew the
little creature into bed.

" Sister, *do* you think so very much of Mr.
Hoyt ? " asked Lina, with her head pillowed
upon Marion's shoulder, which was already
damp with the child's tender tears

" More than I have any way of expressing except through my life-long devotion to him. But I would confess this to none less pure than Lina, — to none else, indeed ! "

" Oh, dear, it's dreadful ! " moaned Lina.

" Do you indeed feel so badly about my leaving you ? "

" I used to feel it all for myself. I guess that was real selfish in me. Now, since he came to-night, I feel it mostly for you ! "

" For *me !* You should have no fears for me, pet. A queen might envy me as the pride of Hoyt ! "

" Marion, *don't* think so much of him ! "

" How you are shivering ! Why, Lina, what is the matter ? "

" Didn't you see it to-night ? Oh, Marion, didn't you ? "

" See what ? " And Marion is alarmed, fearing Lina is losing her senses.

" Him - - do —it ? "

" Do what? Don't rise and stare at me that way! Do lie down! There, drop back upon the pillow, little one. I will bathe your head with cold water ; that will cool it."

"Don't, Marion. I am well enough."

" I should think so. All of a tremble, — white as your dress, — rambling in talk, — and your temples throbbing violently. I must call mother and nurse."

" I am quite well. Let me speak to you! Did you see *him* to-night in papa's library ? "

" Do you mean Warren ? "

" Yes. I saw him there with a number of young gentlemen. Oh dear, they were gay young men. Did you see him there ? "

" Yes ; go on, you strange one."

" They were smoking, chatting, and, oh dear! *drinking!* "

" Wonderful, that last, for the nineteenth century! All gentlemen do that," said Marion, with great composure.

"Not all, sister; papa does not."

"Oh, papa; we expect him to be above everybody."

"Marion, how can you help being serious?"

"Because you are enough so for both of us."

"And I saw Mr. Hoyt," continued Lina in a choking voice, "put a glass to his lips."

"I dare say, Lina."

"Oh, sister! But it seemed as if *he loved it!*"

"Of course he does. Willowglen is famed for its choice wines. Borden can not furnish another cellar like ours. Probably you heard all the young gentlemen said, you precious little eavesdropper!"

"I did, and their talk was all about wines, and such things. Marion, why can't you give him up?"

"I should be utterly miserable without him." And Marion wondered what would come next.

" You may be that, if you marry him, Marion ! "

" Lina, I am growing angry fast. You suggest impossible things. Crying still ? Oh, Lina, your affections and apprehensions will be the death of you ! "

" Don't laugh at me ! I must tell you how much Nurse Collins has suffered," replied Lina, plunging into the story with tears and sighs.

Marion gathered patience to hear her through ; then, nearly smothering her with kisses, she fell asleep.

" She is real pretty. What if she should sometime be a drunkard's wife ! " thought Lina, wide-awake, and leaning over her sleeping sister. " But she mustn't be. I mean to read my Bible, and pray God to keep her happy all her days. And I'll just mention that dreadful story to Warren, and beg him to love

God so much that nothing can go wrong with him."

With these resolutions, Lina slept, while a look of care lingered on her face.

The wedding morn rose bright and clear. The busy household were up with the sun. Happiness reigned supreme but for the shadow that rested on Lina's spirits. Orange-buds, white satin, with floating folds of blonde, the veil sweeping from the graceful head to the floor, the charming blush, the half-concealed tear-drop, the sweet tremulousness of response, rendered Marion more beautiful and charming than ever. Lina, in the thinnest of white muslin, with shoulder-knots and sash of blue satin, and her waving locks of gold, looked very lovely. She was a little troubled how to speak to Warren, even if she could find the opportunity. At last the moment came. Twice the glass had been raised to Warren's lips. Lina had seen it with inexpressible pain. A fresh toast was going the rounds of the board; the well-watched glass was the third time filled, when, —

" Don't, brother ! " came distinctly to Warren's ear.

" ' Brother ' from Lina ! Is this what the ' don't ' is ￟aimed at ? " whispered Warren, lightly indicating the glass.

" Yes, brother ; don't touch it. It makes the very worst of all misery ! People can't always stop, when they once begin with it. Before you go I want to tell you a dreadful story. May I ? "

" Yes, indeed, Lina." Warren tasted no more wine that day.

A few moments before the bridal party left for Saratoga, Lina climbed upon the knee of her new brother, and related the proffered story, and gave good advice, all of which was indulgently listened to.

But, the while, a smile lurked about his mouth, which troubled Lina, who decided, —

"May be, if he don't think much of my story now, he will sometime. I s'pose I was too little to talk to him."

CHAPTER IV.

A BIRTH.

" A babe in the house is a well-spring of joy.'

OT once, during Warren's college life, had the intoxicating glass touched his lips; not once had a game of chance occupied his attention. But he was less careful when he had graduated. The world was glorious and enticing. He had seen little of it till now. His friends — ah! *Marion's* friends — drank, and passed the tempting glass to him.

He was dazzled — yielded! — and Marion, with the ruby poison to her own lips, stood smiling near. This was his first glass. Hereditary fondness repeated that first indulgence. Dariel, who had attended the wedding, left the

festive scene with a heavy heart, as did also
Abel and Dolly.

The bridal party lingered at Saratoga a
month. Upon their return to Borden, many
and gay were the parties made in honor of
them.

" We think your husband quite an acquisition to our family. You must visit us often,"
said a fastidious relative, named Percy, to Marion, whose ingenuous cheek took a deeper blush
at this praise of her husband.

" It will give us pleasure to do so," she answered, casting a fond glance at Warren, whose
attention at the moment was held by as delighted a female relative of hers.

This lady was the wife of her first cousin, a
rather imbecile individual, whom she had married solely to secure and add his fine estate to
her own ample fortune. She was also a cousin
to Percy, the exquisite already mentioned.
She was arrogant and heartless, one who could

not endure to see others prosperous and happy,
not even her own connections. When she had
released Warren, she stood alone, "chewing
the cud of sweet and bitter fancies." Percy
sauntered towards her, and observed, —

"Our little cousin has made a glorious acquisition to our family, Mrs. Umber;" and he
adjusted his eye-glass to take another look at
the happy pair.

"It seems to be a good match, I'll own,
Cousin Percy. But do you imagine Hoyt knows
how to take care of his wealth? One of his
former classmates, — Torrey, — a perfect treasure of a fellow, tells queer stories of Hoyt.
Is he given to drink immoderately? His
father was, you're aware."

"All gentlemen imbibe, Cousin Umber;" and
with a yawn Percy moved away.

"I am tired of this constant party-giving
and going," Warren remarked one day, holding a card of invitation in his hand. "I long

for the *home* in this beautiful spot that I have sighed for from infancy. I don't want Auburn-dale devoted to frivolities." He spoke gravely and earnestly.

" You can not be more weary of frivolity than I am. I long to close the doors on all the world," as earnestly responded Marion. " Shall we ever be together here, alone ? We couldn't weary of each other, Warren."

" Far enough from that last, I trust ! But society will never allow us to try the experi-ment." And Warren's closing words seemed a prediction. The Percys and the Umbers be-came actual bores upon the patience of the Hoyts, bringing with them large parties, for Auburndale was found to be an attraction to the most fastidious stickler for fashion, taste, and refinement.

" Such wines, dinners, horses, etc.!" thought those of the Percy stamp.

" Such agreeable gentlemen !" commented

Mrs. Umber and her daughters, with other females of similar caliber, buzzing about the victimized young couple, who still wondered if their own claims would ever be recognized, and if ever their doors could be closed at their will.

"But you owe something to the world," observed Mrs. Mayburn, at last noticing Marion's displeasure.

"Yet not everything. I think people are very selfish in their demands upon us. Neither of us is very fond of society, at least, such as we have been most favored with. Mr. Percy evidently thinks us nothing but children. He plays high, mother, and drinks frightfully, without getting intoxicated. And the Umbers are fully as disagreeable. Warren's temper and nerves are set on edge by Mrs. Umber's arrogance, boldness, and rasping voice, I know, but he don't utter a complaint, because she and the rest are my relatives. Poor fellow! He has to put up with a great deal on my account. I heartily dislike these people, and am beginning to dread I know not what."

" You are very foolish. It is not often that they honor their young relatives as they have you," said Mrs. Mayburn, in a reproachful voice.

" Because the other young married relatives haven't so much money," interposed Lina, as she sat by Marion's side, industriously making a doll's frock out of a piece of white satin.

" You shock me, Lina! "

" I'm sorry, mamma. I don't want to do that. But the company let out lots of things before me. Mr. Torrey says he means to own Auburndale. I heard him tell Mrs. Umber so; and she laughed, and said he never could do that. Then she said Warren played high, and was reckless. Is he, Marion ? "

" Hush, Lina! You never heard aright. These people have the kindest hearts."

" How can you tell that, mamma?" asked Lina, dropping her work in her eagerness for information.

" Positively, what an odd child you are!"

" Am I, mamma? Please answer my question."

" I can tell they have kind hearts in a multitude of ways, child. Their coming to see Marion so often is one."

" Maybe they come most to see Auburndale. I guess they like it better than they do her, mamma, I do. I often hear them talk out their secret thoughts; they don't mind me, because I'm little, I s'pose."

" Sweet pet! *Do* run out and play in the park. You are with grown-up people too much; you are looking ghostly pale and thin," cried Mrs. Mayburn, astonished and troubled.

5

"I can't stop to play, mamma. Let me fin
ish my doll's wedding dress."

"Whom is she going to marry?" laughingly
inquired Mrs. Mayburn.

"Mr. True, a good young man, who neither
smokes, drinks, plays, nor swears. I hate men
who do; all but Warren, of course."

Marion's eyes were placed full on her chat-
tering little sister.

"Stop talking so, Lina! Run out in the
park and romp with Fido. You are like one
possessed."

"Fido can't talk, mamma; I wish he could;
that is, if he wouldn't talk like Mr. Percy, and
such gentlemen.   Mamma, when I marry, that
is if I live to do such a thing, I shall choose
somebody who has to *work* for a living, for
then *I* shall have to work. He shall know a
great deal about books, pictures, and good people, — so that we may always have something
sensible to talk about. He will not smoke nor

drink. I reckon he *won't!* Nurse says I think just right about it."

" There, that is enough," cried Mrs. Mayburn. But she drew the little head with its clustering curls close to her bosom, and, after kissing the round cheek, looked searchingly into the innocent eyes. Lina was not released until the mother's heart ached with some indefinable foreboding. When the little girl was seen bounding over the lawn, the conversation was renewed.

" Warren and I do not care for the gay world our visitors delight in. I think Lina is nearly right in her conclusions. Besides," — here Marion lowered her voice, — " I fear, mother, that *some* of these visitors *are* unprincipled, that they really *are* planning to ruin us."

" Bless me! how womanly and thoughtful my first-born has grown! Her little heart full of fears for husband, I dare say. What will papa and I do with two such wise daughters, my love?" laughingly replied Mrs. Mayburn, treating her child's confidence as a senseless whim. Mrs. Mayburn's life had been free from anxieties. This we submit as something of an excuse for her thoughtlessness. The remainder of the excuse must come from her broad confidence in everybody with whom she came in contact. She was so easy, amiable, and open-hearted, and generally lacking in discernment, that she did not readily suspect guile in others.

Marion looked hurt, and silently resolved to throw away no more words upon the matter of her surmise, but to watch where she had suspected wrong purposes. Meanwhile, Mr. Torrey, who had adopted the profession of teacher, married a fashionable lady, and seemed so courteous and gentlemanly, and altogether such an entirely different man, that Warren felt obliged to notice him.

" Mrs. Hoyt does not regard us very favorably," remarked one of the *suspected* visitors at Auburndale, at the close of an unusually magnificent dinner-party given at that place.

" She is a young thing; we must teach her a wife's place," sneeringly replied Mr. Torrey, the one addressed, whose dashing wife was afterwards, insensibly to herself, made an assistant of the designing party, and whose hospitality and naturally endearing manners dazzled Marion, and actually charmed her out of her fears.

After this, Marion entered festal scenes with more pleasure, for her "dear friend," Mrs. Torrey, was so delightfully urgent and devoted. This change in Marion pleased her mother.

Alas! that loving mother had forgotten that the truly happy wife is she who in the faithful discharge of her duty finds her greatest earthly comfort and delight. Home is no narrow sphere. In it woman can find exercise for her best, holiest endowments.

About this time, the Misses Umber were married to Messrs. White and Uhland. After a while, they, with Mr. Percy, began to condemn Warren as a " rather *fast* young man." Later, the Hoyts rejoiced over their first-born, whom they named Harvard, but pet-named Harvy. This welcome babe had the spiritual look of Lina, and, like her, early evinced uncommon quickness of intellect. About this dear infant the tender prayers of Dariel clustered. The watchful old man and Mrs. Lumbkin had many secret fears for Warren, who began to grow restive beneath the dread of their deserved rebuke and good advice.

" I fear he will early fill a drunkard's grave, as did his father," often sighed the old man, who had loved the latter as dearly as he did the former.

CHAPTER V.

PARTINGS.

"Oh, that bad ! how sad a passage 'tis !"

NEVER had Marion appeared more beautiful in the eyes of her husband than when bending in enraptured delight over her infant. The picture often moved his susceptible heart beyond measure ; it appealed to one of the deepest and purest emotions of his nature. "My son, my son! How tenderly I will rear him! What may he not become through Marion, blessed Marion, and myself!" was the joyful cry of his love and pride.

And what an important epoch in Lina's life was Harvard's birth! Her head and heart were full of plans in which he was the predominant actor. She had adopted him as her es-

71

pecial care, and not only played with him, but
in the privacy of her apartment constructed
several unique and tasteful garments, which,
we are sorry to record, were scarcely ever
found to fit him in the manner best adapted to
his ease and comfort.

Still she did not despair, but, turning the re-
jected clothing over to some poor child whom
they did fit, went on constructing more, with a
zeal and patience that finally resulted as she
desired. Once, when Harvy was very ill, she
heard Nurse Collins praying for his recovery.

" I too ought to pray that he may get well,"
soliloquized Lina, falling beside her cot, and
pouring forth in artless language a touching
petition.

" I think my babe's recovery is entirely
owing to you, nurse. And I mean to make
you a very acceptable present," said Marion,
when Harvard was fully out of danger.

But nurse would not claim more than her

due, so she replied, looking tenderly upon the unconverted and worldly mother, —

"I did no more than a human being was capable of doing towards getting him well."

"But, nurse, the dear little fellow would not be living if it had not been for you!"

And Marion wept grateful tears, which, dropping upon her infant's face, caused him to unclose his eyes, and smile sweetly upon her.

"Darling one! speak, and tell your good nurse what she is too modest to believe, that had it not been for her, you would not be smiling upon me now!" cried Marion, in a transport of delight and tenderness.

"You mean if it had not been for God," answered nurse, with deep solemnity.

Marion looked at her a moment, then thoughtfully observed, —

"How apt we are to forget Him, or not to

approach Him properly, in our selfishness, prosperity, and ease!"

"Yes, that is too true. But many a petition went up for Harvard's recovery."

"I hope you will always remember Harvard thus."

"I will; but my prayers are not as powerful as Lina's. She is almost an angel now, I think."

"Did Lina pray for Harvy?" with much emotion asked Marion.

"She did, and will never forget him, nor anybody else."

Marion relapsed into thought. She desired to be the best possible guide to her son. Religion had always seemed gloomy to her. Yet Lina, whom she knew by many evidences to be a Christian, was far from gloomy,— was indeed the brightest member of the family. Lina's example could not be lost. Soon her prayers, persuasiveness, and piety attracted her parents to Christ. How different were now Mrs. Mayburn's views of fashionable life!

Harvard was well petted by his grandparents. The distance between them and Auburndale was never so short as now. Margaret, daughter of Nurse Collins, was chosen to attend Harvard, and no more faithful and affectionate being could have been found for the office. Like pleasant dreams a few months rolled on. Warren and Marion were devoted to each other and the child; indeed, so much so that fashionable people saw little of either.

And those few golden months were a developing period to Lina, who drank in grace and instruction as flowers the welcome dew; streams of light were flowing into her soul, calling forth to action every element it possessed. Maturity of thought and expression increased with her, and influenced all about her, not always, however, to the extent she desired. She had never been so happy, for with increased knowledge came intense gratitude that she had been permitted to live in God's beautiful world, and to lift up her spirit on wings of prayer even to Him. This seemed the most wonderful favor of all. In her humility she did not dream how angelic her character was, and sweetly wondered why those about her loved her so dearly.

One bright day in May, Harvard had just finished his first year, and, at her earnest desire, clothed in dresses of Lina's manufacture, was enjoying a drive with his grandparents, nurse, and Lina, to all of whom he managed, by well-known infant signs, to testify his approbation of the undertaking. Lina's demeanor was characterized by her usual sweetness and thoughtful gravity, while her parents were as ever in a state of calm happiness, that ill-fortune had never disturbed, and which religion now heightened.

The air was mild and still, and the woods were quietly busy in putting on their brightest tints. Here and there a bunch of violets tufted the tender grass of the sward, over which the trailing arbutus threw its delicate blossoms and clinging fingers. Glistening among the trees were tasteful summer residences, many of them freshly painted; these, with the unpretending cottage of laborer or inconsiderable farmer; broad reaches of open pasture lands; an occasional church, or school-house, or wooded line of hills, bordered the excellent road that, wide and hard, wound for many a mile ahead. Along the sides of the road, trees had been reared, either by nature or artifice, and now met in arch overhead, and nodded in their own peculiarly graceful way as the breezes played among them, and ruffled the feathers of sundry birds that found shelter among their branches.

"Oh, what a glorious day this is! Papa, I must have a whole lapful of that beautiful arbutus to carry home. Tell John, please, to stop now, as there is a fine lot right here at the roadside," cried Lina.

" Won't it do when we go back ? "

" It may be dark then, papa. I'd rather have it now. Maybe I'd be too tired to gather it then. Please let me get it now."

" You shall have it, pet. But won't you let John get it ? "

" No, papa, it won't be half so pleasant as if I get it. The sward looks like a velvet carpet. I want a good run upon it."

" You shall have a run upon it, so will I. You're a suggestive little body, Lina, and your suggestions are always good ones, — more than can be said of everybody's, that. The spring woods always make a boy of me."

" A run with you, papa, will be nice ! Stop, John ! Ah, I'm out. Oh, Harvard, if you were only big enough to run with us ! "

" He will soon be, pet."

" That he will, papa," cried Lina, soon humming, skipping, and clapping her hands with delight.

They ran, and sang merry snatches of songs, and told stories seated on mossy rocks beneath splendid trees, and gathered many a bouquet.

"Now, papa, I'm ready to drive on," said Lina, whose little hand was furtively pressed upon her side.

"So soon? Why, you're a perfect baby. I could keep the sport going until to-morrow at this time, I know," said Mr. Mayburn, removing his hat to cool his forehead.

Lina did not answer, being intent on hiding the pain in her side from the observant eyes of her mother, — a pain that sadly interfered with her breath.

"What made it come now, of all times? I hope I shan't have to tell of it, as it would spoil all the pleasure of the drive." And Lina, smiling sweetly, crowned Harvard with flowers, while one that she placed in his hand became an object of special curiosity and interest to that young gentleman. The party came upon a woman, wan-eyed, and poorly clad, who was resting by the wayside. She held an infant against her bosom, and upon its little, unconscious face her tears had fallen thickly.

"Why, isn't that Charles Lyle's wife?" asked Mr. Mayburn.

"Yes, poor thing. If she is going our way, perhaps you can give her a seat," said Mrs. Mayburn.

"Oh, yes, we can make room for her," cried Lina.

"Perhaps you'd better invite her, wife."

A look of surprise swept over the faded face, quickly succeeded by a flush of wounded pride. She felt much like rejecting the offered kindness, but sheer fatigue and incipient illness induced her to mount to the seat which Lina had vacated for her.

"You are not looking very well," said Mrs.

Mayburn, feelingly. "Your health is not good?"

"No, ma'am. My health is wretched."

For a moment Mrs. Lyle struggled with her pride. Then she gave it the go-by.

"I'm not much like the happy girl that helped make Mrs. Hoyt's bridal outfit. I've seen sorrow enough since then. Will you please look at my baby, madam? He's just the age of your beautiful grandson. A poor sight is my boy. I was half starved and constantly worried before his birth, and I've been so ever since. Did you ever see a less thriving-looking babe than my Leo?"

"He looks feeble, indeed," sighed Mrs. Mayburn, pressing the poor woman's hand in token of sympathy.

Entirely overcome, Mrs. Lyle poured forth a sorrowful story of disappointment and wrong. Lina wept for many reasons.

Throwing up her arms with a wild gesture,

6

and turning an almost frenzied eye upon Mr.
Mayburn, Mrs. Lyle demanded, —

"Can nothing be done to prevent the sale of
intoxicating drink? Must I and mine and
countless thousands go on suffering torments,
that man's fiendish love of gold may triumph?"

"You ought not to suffer so. The sale of
liquor should be put an end to. Every Christian
on the face of the earth ought to cry aloud to
God to stop this infernal traffic," replied Mr.
Mayburn.

In a strange, hard voice, Mrs. Lyle added,
"Man! I sometimes doubt the existence of
a God!"

"Hush! Don't ever permit yourself to think
that," interposed Mr. Mayburn, dreadfully
shocked.

"You have never seen your daughter, with
that precious, fortunate boy in her arms, shivering with cold, fainting from hunger, while
groveling at her feet lay a drunken husband,

insensible, brutish, careless of their woes, longing, striving only for one thing, — the gratifi-
cation of his love of strong drink. **You** never
heard **a** woman talk **so** before. Your lines
have fallen in pleasant places, and your hearts
— I must add, even if it offend — are rendered
careless thereby. You could do good by learning
the sources of the suffering of hundreds about
you, and exposing them. Do you know that
alcohol produces ninety-nine hundredths of all
the miseries flesh is heir to? It does. Yet you
buy it, offer it to your guests, and never pause
to think what a gigantic evil you are extending
and countenancing by doing so. You look at
me as if you doubted my sanity, and no wonder. **It is** not often my pride will let me speak.
My mother's home is just in view. I'm going
there for food, care, and escape from the brutal
treatment of my husband. I shall soon die, unless I have proper care and nourishment. **My**
mother is poor, but she will minister to her

child's wants. One word more: I give it for Mrs. Hoyt's sake, whom I loved well for her kindness to me when I worked for her. My mother has told me the story of your grandson's paternal grandfather. Of course you have heard of it. Do you know anything of hereditary influences? If you do not, learn, — learn for that baby's sake! Stop here, please. I thank you for your kindness."

"Please take this," whispered Mrs. Mayburn, thrusting her purse into Mrs. Lyle's hand.

"I thank you, and accept it gladly, for I need it," said Mrs. Lyle, with a quivering lip.

"Wife, upon my return, I'll throw away every drop of liquor my house contains," said Mr. Mayburn.

"Oh, do! Alcohol has almost made Mrs. Lyle crazy," said Lina. "It is dreadful stuff."

"I shall look after Mrs. Lyle. She was a happy, capable girl, and was married about the time Marion was," said Mrs. Mayburn.

Agreeing upon a lunch, the party alighted at a cottage, and just as the family were about to partake of an acceptable dinner, served neatly and properly, although delf, pewter, and steel reigned in lieu of porcelain, cut glass, and plate. Lina looked about her with intense delight. She was very democratic.

"It don't take much money to make much comfort, papa," she whispered.

"No, love. Nor industry?"

"A great deal of that, I think, papa. But industry is better than money."

"And dinner just now is better than either, hey?"

"If you please, papa," was laughingly given.

"She's a little thing," said the farmer's wife, noticing that Mr. Mayburn carried Lina in his arms to her seat at the table.

"Hum; I don't know, — about as large as the average," he replied.

"She's only a trifle over eleven," explained Mrs. Mayburn.

The farmer's wife dropped the subject, out of consideration to all concerned, but was secretly glad that her ten-year-old treasure was much larger, and far more healthy.

John, in the mean time, was dining with the farm-hands, among whom, by his superior dress and important airs, he had become quite a lion. At close of dinner, one of the men invited him to a stroll about the place, which he declared couldn't be beat in a circuit of fifty miles.

"What! do you fellows have time for that at noon?" asked John.

His curiosity was silenced by a significant wink from the other. In a few moments the question was answered in a more satisfactory manner to both than John had anticipated. The exhilarating glass touched his lips again and again, ere he left his demoniac tempter, who, in his lair in the hayloft, had commenced a train of evils he little dreamed of.

A pipe filled with abominable tobacco was the next luxury tendered the weak-minded John.

" That will take away the scent of the other. I always like to treat when I meet a rare fellow like you. To be sure, the best I have to offer is poor compared to what you get at your master's. Now, he has the best kinds, I surmise," said the man.

" We have them, but don't use them daily. Not that master's mean, but because he's no fancy that way, and less now than ever. Lately he has joined a church and set up family prayer. Besides, little Miss Lina thinks it's a bad plan to drink, or to have liquors in the house. You ought to hear her talk about religion and temperance! But she won't be here in this world long," said John.

"Of course you never get a taste of those nice liquors, — oh no, of course not!"

John elevated his eyebrows by way of reply.

"You never half drain bottles and casks, and fill them up with suthin' else, I reckon?"

"Water's cheap and handy," observed John.

"I dare say. No harm to cheat your master. He cheats you, I'll make bold to say."

"No, he don't," protested John; "he don't know how. He is a gentleman from the crown of his head to the sole of his foot."

"Maybe some day I'll call down to see you," said the laborer.

John made no reply to the proposition, as the man was too slovenly in appearance and low in behavior and speech to visit at Willow-glen.

Our party were again in the carriage. Soon their progress quickened to furious rapidity. "Papa, how we do rattle along! What makes

John drive so fast? See, it frightens even Harvy," cried Lina.

"Slower, John!" shouted Mr. Mayburn, treating her fears lightly.

"Yes, sir," shouted John in reply, but doing just the opposite.

"Here, papa, please hold my flowers while I look out."

"Certainly, pet, and you too, if you wish."

Lina smiled, and her cheek was met by her father's kiss, as he took charge of her flowers. She looked out, and instantly cried, —

"Oh, papa, how fast we must be going; things fly so! John is driving fast again. He must be careful!"

"John, slower, slower!" again called Mr. Mayburn, who felt no alarm, only discomfort, because Lina was troubled.

"Here come three teams. The road is not wide here, a bit. I don't see how they can pass unless the drivers accommodate. I don't believe John will accommodate. He acts very queer, I think."

" Lina, you are nervous through fatigue. John is a good driver," protested Mr. Mayburn.

" Baby is terribly frightened, sir. We don't go as we came. Coming, the driving was like rocking at home, sir," said Margaret, quite pale and anxious.

Mrs. Mayburn felt secure because her husband did.

" Indeed, we must go slower, or we shall be dashed to pieces. We are close upon those teams, tearing right in among them!" almost shrieked Lina.

" John, be careful! What are you about?" cried Mr. Mayburn, at last noticing aright his daughter's fears. But John dashed on.

" Be careful, John!" shrieked Mrs. Mayburn, holding on by the strap, and half frantic now with apprehension and terror.

An effort to obey was awakened in the

stu_efied driver. Something like a sense of danger animated him to exertion.

Too late, — too late! Shrieks, — a crash, — and groans. Horses and shattered carriages dash over the road. Here and there are moaning beings, in the full abandonment of grief; others there are, all insensible to feeling, not dead, but transfixed and statue-like in despair.

A mangled human heap renders the smooth white road horrible. Lina, Harvard, and Margaret are safe. What of the others? Alas, alas! Once more does the recording angel take up the pen against intemperance, — intemperance. Once more the cry goes up from the gory earth for help, — help to drive to utter annihilation this dreadful scourge.

John lived long enough to make confession.

Mr. Mayburn's head, bleeding frightfully, was resting upon a cluster of the very flowers he had playfully gathered with and for the dear child whom he had often declared he could not live without. Streams of blood subdued their graceful beauty; yet one spray, fresh, unstained, and odorous, with its tender leaves and delicate blossoms, had stretched itself as if with thoughtful care to conceal a cruel gash in the noble forehead. The fond maternal heart had likewise ceased to breathe, to throb a response to child or friend, and in the beautiful face recently full of loving smiles not a single spark of the dear familiar look was left.

Did we say Lina was safe? Can we call that flower saved over whose tender form the tempest has passed with relentless power, until, all stricken to the ground, it lies, not broken, — crushed?

CHAPTER VI

PAINFUL DISCLOSURES.

"But Time went ceaselessly ; joy's rosy hour
  Grew dim with clouds, and storms began to lower.
  New joys there were for him, but grief and pain
  Taught their sad lesson, — never learned in vain."

THE suddenness of the shock that orphaned Lina had left her with one wild wish, — to die.

"You must live for me, dear sister," said Marion, with a look of anxiety.

Marion had not said those words in just that way before. More than two years had gone, since, completely prostrated, Lina had taken to her bed. She thought over those words, and the manner in which they were uttered, until she became fearful of her own imagination. She raised her head in her eagerness to

93

learn the worst. Then, with a quickly-smothered groan, she took in unsparingly every
change in the face of the other. Her searching
eye missed not a single thing. Then, with another quickly-smothered groan, she buried her
face in the pillow, feeling that nowhere on
earth had her worn spirit a home. Fortunately
uprose to memory, then, the last verse her
blessed mother had read and commented upon
to her, — "There shall not a hair of your head
perish." It brought to her new resources of
thought and feeling.

"To-day I will rest. To-morrow I will rise.
No doubt I have been terribly selfish and trying
to sister," she thought, striving to be easy in
mind.

The morrow found her doing her best at
gathering health. Harvard was now over three
years old, very talkative, playful, and happy.
He evidently considered Lina worthy notice,
and trying to amuse. The little fellow suc-

ceeded admirably. Yet shadows and **prostra-**
tion had not wholly left her. The measure
was not full. Once more had Lina's tears to
flow. Her beloved nurse was suddenly seized
with disease that laid her low in the grave, before the child of her loving care had recovered
health. Again was this child fully prostrated
upon a bed of sickness for months.

"I am so much trouble to you, sister. I
have not been **well nor a** comfort since — "
Lina commenced, then, embarrassed, paused.

"Since my marriage," ended Marion, sadly.

"Little Harvard is four years old. Oh, Marion!"

The sisters **wept together.** "Three years
ago!" thought **both. The younger,** seeing
great need of exertion, did her best at getting
up again.

"I think I will go over to Willowglen," she
said quite suddenly one day. She had not
mentioned the place for many, many months.

"Not to-day, the air is so chilly. The wind is east, I think," quickly said Marion.

"Why, Marion, how pale you are! Wl.at can you be thinking of? The wind is not east. There can not be a finer day. But I don't know that I care much about going. Any time will do."

Lina was listless and indifferent enough now. Marion sat with hands wrung together. "Lina," she said at length, with veins swollen like purple cords, — "Lina, I have something dreadful to say to you. Dear, dear little sister!"

Lina plunged her head in the bed beside which she was sitting. Marion was glad to have those intelligent eyes thus hidden. She began: "Warren, poor fellow, hasn't much idea of money nor business. If he had, it would be better for all of us. I have sometimes wished he had been poor when I married him. A great fortune is doubtless an injury to a young man; it gives him too much leisure

time. Lina," and here Marion made a desper-
ate effort to speak distinctly, — "Lina, Warren's affairs are embarrassed, much so, dear."

"Go on, please," Lina murmured, as Marion
paused.

"And Willowglen —" recommenced Marion.

"Not gone from us, sister!" cried Lina,
taking her head from the pillow, with a quick
and dreadful appreciation of matters thus hesitatingly broached.

Marion's streaming eyes said yes; in no
other way did an affirmative come.

"Do not mind it, sister. When I get strong,
I can do something to help myself, — earn
money, I mean. I am not very backward in
my books. People have thought me quite
forward. Maybe I might teach little children," said Lina, without a tear, and most
modestly.

7

" And you have not a word to utter against Warren ! " broke forth Marion.

" He needs our kindest now," said Lina, with her usual discrimination and delicacy.

" Dear, generous, uncomplaining child ! "

" I hear Harvy calling for you, sister," said Lina. Marion crossed to where her sister sat, pale and grave. For one moment the sisters were clasped in each other's arms. When the elder had left the apartment, the younger dared by a certain tearless agony to show her grief.

" Dear papa would not have placed such unlimited confidence in Warren could he have foreseen this. Oh dear, oh dear ! To think I have now no right to enter the pleasant gates of Willowglen ! But I must not seem much troubled when Marion is by. She has enough without that. Oh, if she hadn't married Warren ! "

Soon after, Warren had a conversation with Lina, in which he wished to make it appear that affairs were not so bad after all. She was not deceived, but sat noting the changes in his countenance and bearing. A recklessness of speech, an uncalled-for hilarity, a constant ref-. erence to the opinion and advice of "my good friends Uhland, White, and Torrey," a slovenliness of dress, a shrinking eye, made up a very different being from the man her sister had taken, "for better or worse," not much over five years before.

These disheartening points all characterized the present Warren Hoyt. It mattered not to his pallid listener what he was talking about. She saw that truth, honor, decency, virtue, were fast departing from him. And for Harvard to have such a father! She thought of her own father with fast-coming tears. He had never disgraced nor distressed her. In the midst of her grief she rejoiced over his spotless name. Another source of joy arose from the knowledge that Marion was less worldly.

When Harvard was five years old, he was made very happy by a present of a beautiful pony. This came on a Christmas, with his father as Santa Claus. A pony had long been desired by Harvard, who was a fearless little fellow, and who soon learned to ride on the smooth roads in and about Auburndale, accompanied by Lina on Bessie, a handsome bay mare, — nearly the only remnant of her former wealth and state. This was very delightful exercise to both children. Marion, from the piazza, beheld them depart with pride and pleasure. At six, Harvard was an experienced equestrian. Lina tried to be for his sake. She avoided all roads leading to Willowglen. If, when setting forth on a ride, she rivaled the lily in pallor, she invariably returned rivaling the rose in a warmer hue, but never self-deceived regarding her physical condition.

"Don't Lina look pretty?" cried Harvard

one morning, in admiration of the girl's rare beauty.

Marion's eyes gave her little son all the answer he desired.

It had been a delightful ride to both children. Lina retained her seat in the saddle while recounting in a certain chastened, playful manner everything that had made the ride so pleasant. Her deep blue habit fitted her elegant little figure to perfection. Her black hat with its sweeping feathers contrasted finely with her pure complexion and golden hair. Just enough of color tinged her cheek, while her smile, and sparkling eyes, and ever refined manners and words, made a very sweet creature of her.

Harvard, too, formed a pretty figure in the pleasing picture. He had not dismounted, but sat listening, and looking with bright eagerness at Lina, now and then putting in a word of his own. At last he cried, —

"Mamma, who is that strange man over there by the carriage-house? Has papa a new servant?"

"I don't know," Marion indifferently answered.

"Oh, papa is there too. I wonder why he don't come over here and lift me off, as he always does when he's at home. I'll ride over to him, I think," said Harvard, suiting the action to the word.

The stranger took too familiar an interest in the pony, Harvard thought.

"Papa, what does he mean?" he asked, when, with apparent unwillingness, Mr. Hoyt approached his son.

"Hush, Harvard; don't be haughty and impatient."

"But he talks just as if Jetty were *his*, papa. What can he mean?"

"You've nearly hit the truth, young sir. You may dismount now, if you please. I've a

good ride before me to be done at short notice.
Master's little girl 'll be very anxious to see
her new pony," said the stranger. Harvard
cried, " You shall not touch Jetty. She is
mine, sir. Go away from her this minute ! "

" Pshaw ! I can't dally, boy. Jump down,"
replied the stranger.

Harvard gave one wild look at his father,
whose averted face confirmed the man's story.
Harvard slipped off, threw his whip upon the
ground, and, with one cutting cry of pain,
rushed past his weeping mother, over the splendid stairway, and entered his chamber.

" What is this trouble ? " asked Marion,
when her husband came tardily toward her, in
obedience to her call.

" Nothing, only Jetty is going off," he said.

" Why is she going ? " interrogated Marion.

" Because she can not help it," jocosely answered Mr. Hoyt.

" But why ? " demanded his disgusted wife.

"She has changed owners, that's all. Sometime I will buy Harvy a better pony," replied Mr. Hoyt.

"Oh, Warren, how could you do it?" cried his poor wife.

"Pooh! How foolish to feel so about trifles! We can not always be prosperous."

"True; not if we wilfully drive prosperity from us, husband."

"Pooh, wife! luck will come to us yet."

Marion looked at her husband steadily, then in great weariness ascended the stairs. She lingered outside Harvard's door. Like angel-whispers came the low sweet tones of Lina in gentle efforts at comfort and peace to the heart writhing under its first sorrow.

"Blessings on my sweet sister! I could not do so well as she," thought Marion, with eyes where tears and gratitude were struggling. She did not enter the presence of the children, but went to her own chamber, and sat down to gloomy thought.

"I wonder what sort of a being my wife would have me? She will never forget that little affair," thought Warren, when Marion had left him.

That little affair! It merits explanation, that it may be known how Willowglen became the property of strangers.

The world had looked upon Mr. Mayburn as a wealthy man. Consequently it was surprised to find, upon his decease, that he had been in the habit of hiring large sums of money of Mr. Hoyt.

"Very well," thought the world, "Mr. Mayburn had better have hired of him than of any other man. Mr. Hoyt will never see Lina want."

Marion was as much surprised as the world to learn this fact. Still more surprised was

she to find that Willowglen belonged to Messrs.
White, Uhland, and Torrey.

"How came you to let the estate pass out of
your hands, Warren?" she asked, dismayed.

"Your father owed me, and I owed the gentlemen who now hold the place. I was obliged
to pass over to them certain papers I held,
notes, etc., against your father. I am sorry,
my dear, but it can not be helped We have
Auburndale, Marion."

"See that you keep it, Warren," replied
Mrs. Hoyt, by no means satisfied.

A few days later she was walking in the park,
when she picked up a pocket-book belonging to
her husband. It contained a paper bearing
many copies of one genuine autograph of her
father. Flashes of mental light sometimes re-
veal to us hideous darkness. Her agony was
complete. She had no God, poor Marion, so
she blamed fate. Alas for all of us, who, in

hours of wretchedness, have no God to flee to for comfort, peace, hope!

Her husband a forger! The thought was too horrible to Marion. She never revealed to Lina how culpable Warren had been. The knowledge was nearly madness to herself. Besides, her sister would have been rendered more miserable by the revelation. She saw that Lina understood that somehow Warren had been careless in the management of their father's property, and was content to **let** her think so without desiring to enlighten her as to the extent of his carelessness. Warren **would** not have forged those notes against the living **Mr.** Mayburn. Three evil companions were hunting him down for abominable dues, — debts of honor. These fell hunters he could easily quiet by forging notes against the dead Mr. Mayburn.

Lina never had strength to teach other than **her sister's** children. **But when** able, her

slender fingers assisted Marion in sewing, and
much kind care did she take of the second baby,
James, who arrived in a season of dark fore-
bodings.

And all these changes faithful old Dariel
noted with sorrow and much prayer.   Alas,
how the child of his love had depreciated!
Sometimes Marion, with Lina and Harvy, rode
down to the old man's cot.   Such visits were
always beneficial to Lina, who thirsted to be
with Christ's disciples, and who, sitting close
beside the aged saint, listened eagerly to the
words of wisdom, comfort, and love those
shriveled lips were never weary of dropping.
And how she longed for Marion to turn from
the world to the Father of all light and comfort!
Oh, happy Lina; oh, happy any child who binds
about her heart the word of God: " When he
goeth, it shall lead him ; when he sleepeth, it
shall keep him ; when he awaketh, it shall talk to
him.   For the commandment is a lamp, and

the law is light; and reproofs of instruction are the way of life."

Although little enough money had Lina now, yet she found many ways for the exercise of her charitable disposition. As every day her spirit became more nearly allied to high and holy things, so also was waking up around her a freshly-discovered world of living interest. Often the money for a needed article of dress or comfort found its way into the missionary-box, or about the thin form of some child of poverty; or in sorrow's dwelling it had brought the Word of Life, to root out for evermore darkness and ignorance. One day she had given Harvard a spelling-lesson composed of longer words than he had ever before attempted to learn. One of these, "*aspirations*," seemed to have a peculiar charm for him. When he had mastered the spelling of it, he looked in his dictionary to find its meaning.

" I like the whole of that word," he cried, delighted.

" What word? " asked his youthful teacher.

" Aspirations."

" Do you know what it means, Harvy ? "

" Yes, aunty.   Isn't it a real nice word ? "

" I think it is.   Now give me the definition."

" Aspiration : an ardent wish ; a full pronunciation ; a breathing after."

" That is very well given, Harvy," said Lina, who added, thoughtfully, " Do you remember what Dariel said the other day about the same word ? "

" Yes, aunty.   But I don't believe I should have remembered if mamma had not sighed so heavily while he spoke.   He said, ' To love the world only was a miserable thing, for it was like loving something that could not fail to bring us vanity and vexation of spirit.   Our aspirations should be higher, heavenward ; but instead of setting our aspirations that way, we were apt to set them upon obtaining wealth, state, and other things of earth, earthy.' I know what he meant all the time. He wants everybody to aspire to be a Christian."

"He does indeed. So does every other Christian," said Lina.

CHAPTER VII.

" He from his hereditary nook
Must part: the summons came; one final leave we took."

EXT to James came Grace and Margie,
the tiniest of twins; but not over their
innocence and helplessness did the hopes
of the mother's heart gush forth unchecked by
fear.

By and by, Harvard's nurse not only watched
over him, but extended her loving and sorrowful care to the other children. This happened
when Marion and grief sat side by side through
weary days.

Then a deeper shadow fell. Can we write
it? Alas! Auburndale no longer belonged to
the Hoyts. The man who held the largest

112

claim upon it was Mr. Torrey. Mr. White bought the place to reside upon it. He had also long held a mortgage upon it. Thus, through vicious habits, had Warren Hoyt's paternal home passed out of his hands.

As the four children grew old enough to claim stories from Margaret, she sometimes told them about a beautiful house, filled with everything rich and rare, that stood in the midst of a fine park where magnificent trees nodded their proud heads against the blue sky, in whose thick branches the birds sang all day; of various flowers and clustering vines; of fleet-footed deer, with branching horns and full, bright eyes; of a fine carriage and span, and pony; of pet rabbits, dogs, and squirrels; of sundry playthings costly and curious; of a lake, beneath the shining waters of which dwelt a thousand fishes that darted and played around the merry skiff where were seated her-

8

self, and a certain little boy she could name, and a negro oarsman in gay livery.

And when the three younger children used to clap their hands with delight, and coax Margaret to tell the name of that fortunate little boy, she would turn aside with a saddened face, while Harvard's attention seemed to have fastened itself upon some object far away from the gaze of his little companions. At the close of such narrations, when the children were not minding him, he would steal close to Margaret, and whisper, —

" Don't say over those things again. I can't bear it. It makes the tears come."

Then, as if struck by her thoughtless loquacity, Margaret would clasp him to her heart, and, amid repeated kisses, promise not to wound him again.

To Harvard the remembrance of the happy hours he had spent in Auburndale was an unending regret, and formed a ceaseless longing to live once more within the shelter of the dear walls that he had first opened his eyes upon.

The Hoyts seemed now forgotten by all save Sorrow, who brooded in darkness above them Often Marion longed for the sympathy and companionship of some congenial friend. But none of her former acquaintances noticed her. About her lived people far inferior to any she had formerly imagined existed at all, and whom some strong feeling would not permit her to notice unnecessarily. Lina, as ever, was her greatest dependence. But this dear child was very feeble, and constantly growing weaker.

One day, while indulging in a painful revery, Marion was startled by, — " Bless me, Marion, how can you endure such low walls! Then the neighborhood is so wretched! Why don't you have spirit to declare you will not live here? You — yes, you fairly disgrace the family. It's well your parents did not live to see this. And is it true that you even take in sewing ? "

" It is."

And this was the way Mrs. Uhland first entered the humble home of Marion Hoyt.

Marion's quick tear and meek smile told how much some are called upon to endure in this world.

" Auburndale is so different," rattled on the visitor, daintily gathering up her dashing robes, and refusing the offered chair.

" I can not forget that," sadly replied Marion.

" Do you think our carriage is safe ? The people about here look dangerous. We could not drive to your door because the court is so narrow. Even Peter — whom we bade follow us, and wait below — turned up his nose at the idea of any of our connections living here," said Mrs. White, who accompanied her sister.

These sisters were finely dressed. The children, with the exception of Harvard, had never seen such glittering colors and jewelry, and their eyes and thoughts were consequently fully occupied. They were quite too well-behaved to be troublesome or talkative, but their pretty eyes and innocent thoughts did not lack employment.

"You must come out to Auburndale, and pass an hour or two," continued Mrs. White, with great apparent condescension. "I'd rather you'd come alone, of course, as children are troublesome in strange places, and your husband is a disgrace. I have come to buy your watch, if you will sell it cheap enough. My Aurora is teasing me for one, and so I thought I'd come here, and see what sort of a bargain I could make with you, before I visit the jeweler's."

"And I thought maybe Lina would sell hers to me, as my Fred is also in a great way for a watch," said Mrs. Uhland.

"I will give you ten dollars for yours," said Mrs. White.

"I will give the same for Lina's," said Mrs Uhland.

Both ladies seemed to feel that they were doing wonders of benevolence and generosity.

"We can not dispose of them," said Marion.

"Indeed! I heard you were very poor. Well, we'll give you fifteen dollars apiece then."

"Mrs. White, I have said we can not dispose of them at present."

"Well, then, if it is really so, whenever you wish to, let us know it. I think, judging by the looks of things, you will not be able to keep them long."

Marion closed her lips, and would be what she had ever been,— the ladylike hostess; but her feelings ran riot, threatening rebellion.

Not a sympathetic word, not a gift nor inquiry for Lina, who in her bed-room wept while they were there,— wept for her sister, not herself. Harvard sat on a cricket at his mother's feet; he did not know why, but he wished while those unfeeling ladies were present that he could grow up a man right away. He heard them, in a loud, assured tone, describe the beauties and gayeties of his old home; he saw their scornful eyes and cold glances leveled at his mother, and noticed how contemptuously they kept aloof from the inmates of the lowly home they had entered only to render it more miserable; and wished, with a strange wild throb of revenge, that an earthquake would come and swallow them.

When they had gone, Lina called to her sister. Marion went into the bed-room, and was shocked to see how bright were Lina's eyes, and how deep the hectic on her cheeks.

"I am glad you did not sell your watch to those ladies, for I do not think they offered you a fair price."

"You are right, darling. And so you heard

them,— all that they said, very likely. I wish
the walls were thicker, for you are often
obliged to hear unpleasant things."

"Do not worry on my account, sister; I am
comfortable enough. Do you know what the
watches are really worth?"

"Not far short of their original cost. Our
parents gave one hundred dollars for each.
Ten dollars was a great offer for them, pet!"
replied Marion, quite ironically for her.

"But when we do need to part with them, we
will, without a murmur, sister. After all, a
body can do without a watch," said Lina, with
a smile that drew tears into Marion's eyes.

"More than human, almost divine," murmured the wretched wife, smoothing Lina's
hair.

"I hope, sister, you will not hesitate to sell
mine, whenever you need to. We must not
let our little ones suffer for anything while I
have it. Perhaps you had better keep yours as

long as possible; something of better fortune
may turn up for you, — who knows? . In that
case, Harvard would like your watch. I think
you will see brighter days."

"Oh, Lina! Lina! The comfort that you
are!"

"Not so very much, I think. But, sister, I
want you — I want you to think less of me.
You know earthly idols are — don't cry, Marion! — are apt to be broken."

"I do, sweet one. But may God spare me
my idol long!" sobbed Marion.

That evening, when Warren came home, he
angrily told Marion that "her cousin, that per-
fumed sneak, that fair-weather friend, Percy,
had cut him, actually cut *him*, and that, too, in
the presence of a score of old acquaintances
who were once glad to turn up at — the old
place down there."

And speaking of "the old place," that hal-
lowed spot, that Eden from which, like Adam,

for his own sin, he had been ignominiously driven forth, always gave poor Warren the blues, an aching heart to Marion, and to Harvard countless tears shed in secret. But Lina's temper was of higher birth.

Not many months had gone by ere the watches were sold to a man who talked in such a way to Marion that she thought herself very lucky to get eighty dollars for both. This sum bought many needed comforts for Lina and the children.

Once, when at a common eating-house Mr. Hoyt had imbibed a worse quality of wine than his former cellars had ever dreamed of, he dressed himself with scrupulous care, and, taking Harvard by the hand, avowed his intention of dining at the Umbers'. In vain Marion implored him not to think of it, and in vain Harvard protested he did not wish to go ; the poor man was bent on further disgrace to himself and family.

" I will go! " exclaimed Mr. Hoyt. " I have not been to a dinner-party for an age. Umber gives one to-day, I hear. As he never sees any of us, he is not to be blamed for forgetting to invite us."

" If he wanted to invite us, he would ; that is, if his wife would permit him. She long ago dropped us, Warren."

" Cease, Marion. I find Mrs. Umber is not the only woman desirous of ruling her husband. I shall go, for I find the people about here do not quite understand the immense gulf between them and me. Just now, that plebeian penny-postman, that clumsy Abel Lumbkin, actually slapped me on the shoulder with all the assurance of an equal on the most familiar terms, while his ' Hullo, old feller ! ' rang out on the foul air like rolling thunder. I scorned to touch the creature, but I trust my look sent him back to his ignoble sphere."

" Mr. Lumbkin is a real good man," broke

in Jimmy. "He is, for he gives his children nice things to eat and wear and play with. They let me go into their house often."

If James's belongings had been anywhere but in that poor home, he would have been hastily driven to them by the indignant gaze Mr. Hoyt fastened upon him. If silenced, the boy's thoughts were busy with the desire to find in what particular Abel Lumbkin was unworthy to address his father. He did not immediately discover the truth. It was a bitter moment when he did. For respect and affection for so weak and erring a parent held, with a kind, lingering unwillingness to leave their hold upon his judgment when it was correctly drawing the line, and showing Abel Lumbkin to be the better, more worthy man of the two.

Marion's heart ached as she saw Harvard go out with her unfortunate husband. He tried to look and act the hero for the sake of the dear, patient mother so sorrowfully watching him.

"Just now I met Warren Hoyt, and spoke to him, meaning to urge his signing the pledge. But he shook me off with scorn. It 'pears to me the lower he gets, the haughtier he treats his old true friends. He don't often visit Dariel now. I think if he had died when his mother died it would have been better for a heap of folks, Dolly."

"It seems so, I confess, Abel. But God knows best."

CHAPTER VIII.

'" My child is yet a stranger in the world."

"WHAT presumption!" groaned Mrs. Umber, when into the presence of a large party the inebriated Hoyt, dragging his humiliated son, thrust himself, reeling and grimacing.

The unfortunate man tried to make himself agreeable by absurdly shaking hands with and addressing a few immaterial remarks to every person present, whether they had previously met or not.

"Mr. Umber, bestir yourself. Think of some way of getting rid of the creature," said the mistress of the feast in a terrible whisper to her husband.

126

"Hey? Get rid of Hoyt? I thought you liked him. At least, you used to go down to his place often. A pretty place it was too; prettier than it is now, for all White and Torrey have cut down here and stuck in there. But that's because Torrey and White haven't the taste of the Hoyts!" replied Mr. Umber, half dreaming, and half in perplexity what to do with his unwelcome guest, and, last of all, decidedly offended with his wife for her heartlessness.

"He must be taken from the company."

"I see that, wife. But what a pity he happened to come in just that plight, when he used to be so welcome here! And what a pity he lost Auburndale!"

"He lost it because he played and drank deeply. You know what Mr. Torrey told us his tastes even in youth were. So don't ramble into the past, now."

"Mrs. Umber, it is my private opinion that

Torrey is a liar and a knave. I'm glad I've no more boys for him to tutor. You engaged him for our son, wife. If he's ruined, it won't be my fault."

" What a goose! Has all your talk anything to do with the matter in hand ?" said the lady.

" What would you have me do ?" and Mr. Umber raised a penitent and rather humble look at his wife, who towered indignant and haughty above him.

" Do ? When will you ever learn to think for yourself? Take him into your private smoking-room, and give him cigars and wine in plenty. Keep him there at any cost. I'll send the boy into the kitchen. Go at once."

" How quick you are to think, wife !"

The next moment Mr. Umber had ambled to the side of Mr. Hoyt, and whispered,—

" Suppose you and I have a private smoke

in my sanctum. It is a long time since we met."

"I sha'n't stir from this spot. You want to drive me off. I've come to dine here," was the dogged reply, as Hoyt moved away, and, with a shadow of his once fascinating manner, strove to make himself acceptable to all present.

"Of course," interposed Mrs. Umber, following him. "but as we shall not dine for an hour, wouldn't you enjoy a cigar first?"

"I see through you, woman. You want to get me out of the house. I never treated you so when you used to visit me. I sha'n't stir!"

With this, Mr. Hoyt measured his length on a brocatelle lounge of exquisite workmanship.

"Husband, wouldn't you like Mr. Hoyt's judgment upon that lot of wine?" continued Mrs. Umber, nearly in despair.

"If he will oblige me so much," replied Mr. Umber, mentally chuckling over his wife's superior wit, yet as much ashamed of her want of feeling.

"I'm willing," said Mr. Hoyt, putting his arm through Mr. Umber's, and stumbling from the room.

"How dreadful! Who would think that wreck could be the once elegant and courted Warren Hoyt!" murmured Mrs. Torrey. This lady possessed quick but rather inactive sympathies. "Why," she continued, "they say that his wife is quite broken down, poor thing, and actually takes in sewing!"

"Better never be rich than allow extravagance to ruin you," sententiously said Mrs. White. "Borden hasn't other estates within its suburbs equal to what theirs were."

"Mr. Hoyt was more sinned against than sinning," said Mrs. Moreland, a lady whose kind glances had often wandered to Harvard, who, with flushed cheeks and air of painful embarrassment, showed that his feelings were keen and sensitive.

"Now, Mrs. Moreland, just as if he couldn't have kept up in the world if he had been anxious to! I must say, though, Marion was to blame for allowing him to run such lengths. She was a very extravagant creature," interposed Mrs. White, in a harsh, decided tone.

"Not extravagant for one of her supposed means," said Mrs. Moreland.

"Both were to blame for their downfall," persisted Mrs. White.

"I can not think Mrs. Hoyt was; nor was her husband, primarily. I would not be the one, nor have that one connected with me by ties of consanguinity, who got him intoxicated, and then played Willowglen and Auburndale out of Mr. Hoyt's reach," replied Mrs. Moreland with a visible shudder. Her quick flush the next moment showed that she remembered that she might have touched an unpleasant chord. Mrs. White blushed and attempted a reply. Mrs. Torrey stroked nervously the folds of her satin dress, and then said,—

"The habit of gambling is dreadful. I mean to teach my boys to hate cards, and all sorts of games."

"That is a good resolve. Teach them also to shun the designing and unprincipled," said Mrs. Moreland.

"You would also prohibit the wine-cup?" scoffed Mrs. White. "I believe you advocate temperance."

"Assuredly. I would hang in their sleeping and play rooms, as a motto to be never disregarded, 'Taste not, touch not, handle not.' We can not too faithfully guard the precious lambs committed to our trust. Do you teach your children the value of the Bible? If you do not, I pity them and you. The young of the present day are not as familiar with it as they were in that golden time when, pillowed in the arms of my pious mother, I heard in persuasive tones from her lips how holy and priceless a gift it was. Alas! how early and sadly missed was that dear parent! But her lessons sunk deep in my heart. How often she said to me, ' Unless our deeds have a foundation in Christ's wisdom and love, they have no sure hold.' I know we are all blind by nature, but the light, the imperishable, God-given light, can penetrate the deepest darkness."

Mrs. Torrey looked grave. Mrs. Moreland's words reminded her of a time when she, too, had been taught the truth by lips long ago silenced. Mrs. White moved away with an ill-concealed yawn ; she had no remembrance of a period when the Bible had been held up as a fitting guide and friend for her.

When Harvard entered that gay room, and encountered so many surprised, cold, and contemptuous glances, the lightning of passion shot through every vein. He had left his sad mother with a desire to feel and act the hero, and this, with intense effort, he had been able to do, as long as he remained within the range of her anxious eye. After that, his spirits sank to their old level,—the level he always groveled in when his father, intoxicated and careless, insisted upon making a disgusting spectacle of himself. And this the fallen man often did. Harvard was almost beside himself as he dropped his eyes, after his first hasty and comprehensive survey of the proud guests. One wild wish for a hiding-place filled his thoughts Wounded pride, injured feeling, a present dreadful disgrace in the person of his father, the remembrance of his mother's distress, and the wonder what would be the end of this rencontre, filled his eyes with raining tears, and his little form with convulsive sobs. His heart seemed bursting with passion and pain when he heard the comments of the company, not half of which we have repeated, the whispered conversation of the host and hostess, conducted near him, and beheld his father turned out of the room. Then, like a ray from heaven, came the welcome voice and words of Mrs. Moreland. Harvard raised his eyes to take a full if furtive survey of the benevolent-looking and plain-spoken elderly lady.

Tears were rolling down his cheeks, but his gaze was fastened on her as she spoke, for a furtive glance had not satisfied him. There was one, then, in the wide world, whose frankly-expressed opinion chimed with the unspoken thought that had burdened many a revery of his. This revelation was partial peace to him. His violent excitement left him, but over his young face settled an expression of mingled sadness and thought, sorrowful to witness on one so childlike in years and stature. And in all save feeling Harvard was a very child. Sorrow had denied him rightful growth of size and strength, but had greatly developed his perceptions.

Then came a word in the cold, harsh tones of Mrs. Uhland. It chilled Harvard more than any other had been able to. Could it be a true one? All of a sudden he felt so weak that he caught hold of a chair to support himself. Still he must listen to the story, — listen to the close.

"In a consumption? Poor child! She always had a delicate look, quite unusual to youth. Ah! her fate would have been far different had her sister never married Warren Hoyt! I remember when she was the pet of the household. She was lovely, considerate, and winning, — a most rare, sweet child. Ah, well! none of us can say what we may come to," replied Mrs. Moreland, the lady addressed.

"We may all safely calculate on an end far different from Lina's," said Mrs. Umber, in a light, indifferent way, that sent the blood rushing through Harvard's veins, while his brain seemed on fire and his heart bursting with this fresh, unanticipated sorrow.

"What! Lina die! What would become of us all were such a dreadful thing to happen?" inly groaned Harvard, who, in his eagerness to hear, had emerged from the corner, where, half-hidden by a Psyche, he had entrenched himself upon his entrance.

"Mercy! how that boy is watching us! Is it possible he did not know Lina was ill? I am sorry he has heard of it here. I fancy before this information he hasn't had the pleasantest time of it," said Mrs. Torrey.

"I fear he had not heard of it before. How haggard he looks! But how else can the child of an inebriate's home look? I must seek out his mother; I am glad, while looking at him, that nothing but ignorance of her place of residence has kept me from her," thought Mrs. Moreland, going to Harvard, and addressing a few words to him, striving to lighten the evident depression of feeling under which he was laboring.

It was of little use. He could not forget what he had heard with horror. The bolt had descended, and never again could its corroding weight be removed.

Mrs. Torrey, also, tried to charm him into a different state of feeling. She could not, for poor little Harvard remembered many unpleasant things against her husband. Mrs. Umber saw these ladies gathering about Harvard, and did not like it. "They are only curious to find out all they can of Marion's poverty, just to humble me," she thought, for she was no believer in sympathy for the lowly, or disinterested benevolence. She hurried off to learn why he had not been taken to the kitchen, as she had directed.

CHAPTER IX.

"If erst he wished, **now** he longed sore."

THEN came a servant and took Harvard below, where she heaped upon him cake and fruit in such quantities that he wondered if there could be any left for the company up-stairs. It was well for Sally Horne that her mistress did not witness such reckless generosity. But Sally was anxious to make amends for what he had suffered.

"Why don't you eat, sonny?" asked Sally, kindly. She knew his history, for the news the parlor discusses always takes flight to the kitchen.

"You are very good; but I don't want any thing."

139

"Kinder lonesome, hey? In course you are! Childern allus are, leastwise mostly, unless they have childern to play with."

And off Sally darted, and soon returned with a sweet little girl, a year or so younger than Harvard.

"Here's a companion for yer. She's a nice one, an't she? Now fall to, and enjoy yourselves!" cried Sally, after carefully closing the door behind her.

But the children stood looking at her, or awkwardly glancing at each other.

Harvard saw, in the rich attire and costly ornaments of the little girl, only an extension of the dividing line that had commenced so unfeelingly in the drawing-room. And the little girl beheld in Harvard the saddest-faced boy she had ever met. At present they could not mingle. Sally looked on with great dissatisfaction. "Aurory, why don't ye say suthin'?" she asked, with a perplexed sniff.

" I can't, Sally."

" My! Can't ye tell this little gentleman that yer name's Aurory White," said Sally, anxious to beat up a conversation between the two, " and that ye live down in a splendid place called Auburn — well, no matter where ye live, — what an old fool I am ! — and that ye own a pony all black except one or two white spots, — "

" Yes, indeed, Sally ; and that it once belonged to a little boy named Harvard Hoyt," interposed Aurora.

" Massy sakes ! I didn't know that," thought Sally. " I'm allus a blunderin', 'tickerlarly when I don't mean to."

" Now, this Harvard Hoyt," continued Aurora, talking to our hero.

" Never mind who the pony belonged ter," broke in Sally.

" It does, though, Sally, because Harvard

was once rich, very rich, but his papa and his mamma made him poor — "

" His mamma didn't, I know," interposed Sally; for which Harvard gave her a thankful, if a very sad smile. He did not feel able to say a word. . His little heart was full.

" It must be so," gently replied Aurora, " for my mamma says so; and she also says that I must be very saving and prudent, or maybe I shall be just as poor as he is now. Mamma thinks there's nothing so good as saving. But I think there's something better."

" You do, Aurory? What can it be ? " said Sally, as she stroked the silken locks with a loving hand.

" Can't you guess, Sally ? " shyly asked Aurora.

" Not if I tried a month, Aurory."

" Can't you, little boy ? " asked the fairy, with a timid air.

To her, Harvard seemed very wise, because

of his still, sad ways. She repeated her question.

Harvard smiled, but did not otherwise answer. He did know of something which he thought better than saving.

"You see he can't, so ye'd better tell us," urged Sally.

"It's giving," said Aurora, with very, very round eyes, and a peculiar air of delight and mystery. "You needn't tell mamma of it; but when I am a woman, won't I give to everybody that needs, whether they ask for it or not! that is, if I have anything to give. I guess you'd do just so, little boy. So would Sally. My, how she does give her earnings to the needy!"

"You'll allus have suthin' to give, Aurory."

"Shall I, Sally? Are you sure?"

"Sure as I'm alive."

"Oh, Sally, how glad I am!"

"It mayn't be money, Aurory."

"May not be money? What can it be, then?" asked Aurora, in great amazement.

"Sweet smiles and gentle words, honey! I've seen them, many a time, go furder than money. Nobody can take them away from ye, for they're yer very life, and nothing short on't. Now, Aurory, let me drop this ere word in your ear, and in your'n too, little man: never be sparing of that ye can give, and no loss to yourselves. And its masterly good to sacrifice, too,—to raise an altar and lay thereon all that can be spared from the outside and inside, not reservin' to ourselves fatness, or the cause of fatness, for the Lord loveth the cheerful giver, and never takes more than He can give; and, yes, childern, never takes what don't belong to Him. Mind that, now, and bestow freely."

Before Sally had ceased speaking, Harvard, as well as Aurora, was sheltered in her arms.

After a few mutual embraces and kisses, Sally separated the children, momentarily retaining Harvard for the purpose of whispering, —

" Ye needn't let out to her what your name is; it would half kill her if she knew she'd been talking yer up, right afore yer face. Nor ye needn't tell yer ma, neither; it's no use makin' folks feel uncomfortable for nothin'. To do so shows ignorance, or a want of our good Lord's grace in the heart. So keep it to yourself."

" Does she live where I used to?" asked Harvard.

" Yes. But don't lay it up agin her. It's none of her fault. She's an angel. Just look at her! How such a hard couple come to have that lump of pure gold gin 'em is more'n I can imagine," replied Sally, as Aurora took it into her happy head to pirouette over the brick floor.

" Aurora! Aurora! Where can you be hidden?" cried a trio of joyous voices, as a fresh instalment of undimmed childhood lighted up the homely, ill-furnished kitchen.

" Who is that fellow ? " demanded the foremost child, a short, thick-necked boy, not yet out of frocks.

" My friend ! " gayly answered Aurora, floating up to Harvard, and wreathing her arms around his neck, mingling her sunbeam tresses with his dark locks.

" I guess so. Look at his clothes ! Why, he's real poor ! Let's drive him out. I guess he came a-begging. Come, let's hunt him out of the premises ! "

At these insulting words Harvard started forward ; but instantly following him, and placing her tiny hand over his mouth, Aurora cried. — " Don't speak a word, little fellow. Now just go away, Fred Uhland, or else my friend may do something awful to you. Maybe he'll shoot you. I shouldn't wonder, there ! You couldn't blame him, if he did."

" Why, children, how came you down here, of all places in creation! I missed your noise from the nursery, and that's why I've hunted you up. Aurora is actually hugging that low boy!" cried Mrs. Umber, suddenly appearing at the door. Then, in sterner tones, she added, —

" Grandchildren, go to your play-room, and don't leave it again until you are bidden. Boy, you can wait here till your vile father sees fit to take his departure, or go now, as you please."

" I shall not leave without him. It would not do," replied Harvard.

" Very well. Only be sure never to enter my doors again. Your mother must have put you both up to coming. That's no way to gain our notice, I can tell her."

" She did not want us to come; indeed she did not! Father would, and made me come, too."

" Humph! Come, children, come." And

the haughty woman drove the little ones out, but not until Fred had caught up a piece of brick from the broken floor, and sent it with force at Harvard's head.

Seeing this, Aurora darted back, and pressed a kiss upon the wound, a drop of blood from which deepened the coral of her sweet lips. She did not know of this acquisition, but Harvard did.

His eyes filled with tears as they followed the fairy in her swift flight from the apartment, for Mrs. Umber had dared to lay a harsh hand on the delicate neck, that blushed as if with shame for such coarse manifestations from one whose constant boast and gratulation was, "I am a lady."

"The temper! To strike that darling! There, don't stir, Harvard; you would be but a mouse in the cat's grasp. I'll tell Aurory, however, that ye wanted to come to her rescue. They'd better mind; she may fly away from them some day," sobbed Sally, as she engaged vehemently in the drudgery on hand to drive away her distress.

"I could — I could — " commenced Harvard, in angry excitement, and with clenched fists.

" Attack the wicked woman, I s'pose. But, my child, it would do no good," interposed Sally, resting on her broom-handle, the better to survey the child's face as she spoke. " God will make it right, though."

Harvard sat down, thoughtful and heavy-hearted enough for one of mature years. This gloom did not last long. He would not have it so.

" Wal, what conclusion have ye come ter ? " inquired Sally, again resting on her broom, having swept everything out of its place but Harvard, under whose chair her keen eye had caught sight of a few straggling particles of dust.

Harvard smiled, but did not answer in any other way. He could open his mind with the high resolves it had formed to none but his mother. Yes, there was one other, — he thought of her with a sigh, — one so good and unfailing; she must know too. Perhaps it might help her get well to see him hopeful, and strong in a good purpose; at any rate, if at any time he gave up in despair through disappointment, she should never see it. He would guard his face and speech in her presence. He now noticed that Sally was growing uneasy. He soon saw why, as she kept glancing under his chair.

"I would have moved before if I had known I was in the way," he said, apologetically. His respectful manner delighted and gratified Sally.

"Ye're a good boy. Ye'll see luck yet, or Sally Horne is no prophet. Be pertickler to honor yer mother, and father too. Parents are

parents, let 'em be what they will. I know, for
I lost mine airly in life."

After saying this, Sally bathed and bound up
his head, finished her sweeping, and told him
stories while polishing her silver. Well-dressed
servants of both sexes occasionally entered the
kitchen, but were quite too high to notice our
hero except by a hasty glance.

Mr. Hoyt did not announce his readiness to
return to his anxious wife until late in the
evening. Being summoned to attend him,
Harvard found him sitting on the granite steps,
the street-door closed and locked behind him,
and a basket hanging on his arm. With some
difficulty he arose, and said,—

"Why, my boy, how came you to leave this
stately mansion by the servants' door? A relative's mansion,—a right noble relative too.
Harvard, you are too humble. I'm ashamed
of you. Go up the steps, ring the bell, enter
the hall, and take proper leave of your kind un-

cle and aunt, then come out of the guests', not the servants', door.   Come, go at once, my son. I'll sit down again, and wait for you."

"Father, not for the world! I heard the porter slam and lock the door behind you as I came along. They have all had enough of us, father. Can not you see it?"

"Why, what a jealous little pate! We were right welcome guests, I tell you. I did not see much of you, but of course you were well cared for."

"Oh, father!" sighed Harvard, helping him to his feet. No easy task was it to do this.

"What now?" asked Mr. Hoyt sharply, throwing off his son's hand, and endeavoring to walk with dignity and grace.

"Nothing." Harvard saw it was of no use to talk much to his father then.

. "What have you in that basket?" he asked, perceiving how carefully his father carried it.

"Oh, fruit, cake, and bonbons for your dear

mother and the children. Here, Harvy, take it, but carry it straight, if you can, which'll be more than I am able to, owing to a weakness in my legs, I suppose. Won't they be glad of it? What fine people the Umbers are, particularly Mr. Umber, who would not rest until he had engaged me in a confidential chat in his own private sanctum, — a splendid apartment, by the way, such as I used to have, heigho! — and mean to have again, — and made me pass judgment upon a lot of new wine. And I had my dinner there, too. I believe I went to sleep after I had eaten. When I awoke I found myself alone in the room, and not feeling quite well enough to hunt him up, I made myself at home among the luxuries at hand. When your over-fastidious mother knows how much we've enjoyed ourselves, she'll not object to our coming again, will she?"

"I never will come again, father!"

"Harvy, Harvy! how ungrateful!"

"They did not want us here, father," the boy could not help declaring.

"They did, Harry. Don't be jealous, sonny."

Harvard found it of no use to overthrow the disgusting self-complacency of his father. He was glad the walk home was long. The evening afforded no facilities for riding in that direction. Mr. Hoyt must of necessity become more sober the longer he exercised in the clear, frosty air. This he evinced by becoming more clear in ideas and speech, while the "weakness of his legs" was visibly decreasing.

Now was Harvy's time.

"Father, let me throw away the stuff in this basket."

"What ails the boy! Mrs. Umber — or Cousin Umber, as I ought to call her — filled it with her own hands. Do you hear? Throw it away? Here, pass the elegant toy to me. I am not ungrateful. I am not so mean and selfish as to wish to deprive others of unexpected pleasure. Besides, I asked her to give it to me. That step toward doing something for a living will please Mrs. Hoyt. Will it not, my son?"

"Father, do let me throw the basket away!"

"I shall not. 'Willful waste makes woful want,'" said Mr. Hoyt, snatching at the basket.

"Father, do hear me! Don't let it be said that the children, and precious Aunt Lina, and mother, dear mother, ate the leavings of a feast they were not thought good enough to be invited to!"

This appeal had the desired effect with Mr. Hoyt. Somehow it penetrated beneath his drunken sense of matters, and reached his heart Leaning against a lamp-post, with the back of his hand he wiped away a few maudlin tears, and muttered incoherent regrets at his "confounded ill-luck," as Harvard opened the cover, and threw the basket with its offensive contents over a wall separating a lot from the highway. And then, to Harvard's, consternation, he drew a flask from his pocket and applied it freely to his lips. This too, Harvard feared, came from the house they had left. By the time they had reached home, Mr. Hoyt was unfit for any spot but his bed, to which Marion lighted him with much of the tender care of former days, wishing to shield him from the angry eyes of Margaret.

But Harvard lingered in the simple parlor to relate some of the events of the day, and to cheer his listeners with just as much of a bright story as he could make out of the whole. Sally was highly lauded and admired by all. He told them, too, of the fairy child whose joyous presence and generous protection had made her a very Aurora to him. But he could not speak of the warm indignant kiss, nor the proof of her beautiful sympathy that her pure lips bore away.

This was a secret he hid far out of sight, in the holiest chamber of his heart. None should kr.ow it but himself. It was wealth to him; not above, but apart from that he held in the gentle being who called him son; and in that of her who stroked his face, and bade him in a faint voice " never forget Lina ; " in that of the almost fatherless little ones who called him brother, yet looked up to him with almost the reverence and affection of children.

How thin had grown Lina's cheeks, how hollow her temples, and feeble her voice! Harvard noticed all this, as he chattered of his visit. When he left her to go to his room, he knelt beside his couch, and begged with streaming tears that her days might be long in the land, — long enough to enjoy the fruition of ennobling aspirations born of that hard day.

Long before this hour, Mrs. Umber had charged her family and guests not to tell Aurora the name of the meanly-clad boy who had come uninvited and unwelcome.

"She is a strange child; has no sort of

pride; and such a passion for the poor! It would kill her to know his name. She would pine in the house after knowing he had lived there in luxury before her," said the heartless woman, who added, "The other children had better not be told his name, as they would be apt to tell her."

CHAPTER X.

DARKER DAYS.

"Famine is in thy cheeks,
Need and oppression stareth in thine eyes."

TWELVE months dragged wearily on. Denser clouds gathered about the Hoyts. Margaret went away to enter a home of her own, better than that she left; and, as means were lacking to furnish help in her stead, Marion's own hands were obliged to perform the most menial offices, with such assistance as her children were able to afford her. Mr. Hoyt had become a burden as well as disgrace to his family, and often drained the scant earnings of his wife and Harvy to indulge in low gaming and betting, or to spend in ale-houses. Ah, and he did not hesitate to murmur at hav-

159

ing Lina to support! This was worse than all
the rest to Marion. During this period of sorrow, Harvard was rapidly developing. He saw
how much it became his duty to assist his uncomplaining mother, who had chosen Christ to
be her support. He did not grow restive under the responsibility this conviction presented.
Shades of care, annoyance, and displeasure
often rested on his face — indeed, the first
never left it — upon witnessing the conduct of
his father, but seldom did a harsh word, never
a complaining one, drop from his lips. He
quietly drew in countless lessons from the example of Lina. As far as possible, in the
presence of his mother a state of calm happiness seemed to pervade him. He helped, encouraged, and cheered her; entertained the
children; and unconsciously, by the force of
his own example, taught them to be hopeful,
energetic, persevering, and patient. But there

were hours when, unseen, the child's assumed strength gave way.

"'Taste not, touch not, handle not," in letters made of scraps of colored leather, with an ornamental border of the same material, hung at the foot of the bed in which Harvard and James lay. Every morning the eyes of both boys took in these words before any other object.

"If that sign *didn't* hang there, I never would touch a drop of any kind of intoxicating drink. I guess Mrs. Moreland's little folks never knew what drunkenness was, or she might see some use in hanging up such words," said James, upon first beholding the motto.

"But, Jimmy, we can not be too safe. Don't you remember our minister's text last Sunday was, — ' Let him who thinketh he standeth take heed lest he fall"? So aunty says our dear heavenly Father must have seen the need of constant watchfulness, or he would not have put those words in his Bible, little brother."

11

"No, indeed! But you needn't fear for me, Harvard. If I thought I should ever be a drunkard, I'd fall right down on my knees here, and pray God to take me straight at once to Him."

Not long after this conversation, the motto was carefully taken down, and carried to a humbler home, where again it occupied a position at the foot of the boys' bed; but the wall against which it hung was neither lathed nor plastered; and the light by which it was seen came in feebly through three panes of glass. The remainder of the window-frame had adopted wood and tin instead of glass. It was a poor tenement. Distress is ever the atmosphere of the inebriate's home. But Harvard put the best face upon their present abode, for the sake of his mother, to whom he said, buoyantly,—

"Mother, I think we can see more of the sky here than we could at the other home. That is always a pleasant sight, especially when the

sun shines or the stars are out. Even when
there is a storm, the sky is grand and wonderful. Last night I came to this window, and
what should I see but the beautiful full moon,
right there, beaming down upon me! Oh, how
happy it made me! Mother, I don't think people ought to feel badly, no matter what troubles them, if they can see the moon and stars
and sun and sky. **Do you?**"

"No, indeed! And **I** don't think a certain
woman I could name ought ever to feel badly,
when she has such a hopeful, strong young
spirit to help her along." And with this, Marion strained Harvard to her breast, then bent
her head upon his shoulder, breathing an inau-
dible prayer for his continued growth in every
good and perfect thing.

Before Harvard had praised the meager
home, the children were sitting about in great
discontent. They missed their former pleasanter home, and especially their playmates,

the little Lumbkin children. But Harvard's hopeful words, and the impulsive embrace of their mother, awed and subdued them into a different state of feeling, until they too began to see beauties where they had beheld only deformities.

"I will sell pea-nuts between schools, mother, if you are willing. It is quite a profitable business," said Harvard, merrily showing a dime that he had earned by holding a gentleman's horse. The kind maternal smile encouraged him to proceed.

"This, added to what I got yesterday for helping Mr. Brown clear up his store, will make twenty-five cents, — quite a capital to begin with. I can purchase the pea-nuts about the wharves cheaper than at the stores."

"But I dread to have you enter such places, my son," said Marion, in the fullness of a mother's loving anxiety.

"I can take care of myself. You have taught

me how," Harvard answered in a confident tone, while the bright, **earnest** face spoke the firmness of character his poor father had ever lacked.

At first, this business **of selling** pea-nuts promised well. Indeed, Marion was often surprised and pleased at the little hoards Harvard nightly tossed into her lap.

James's efforts at errand-going helped swell the daily income, for the example **of the** older brother was **not, could** not be lost upon the **younger, and the little** fellow, although often sorely tempted, **bravely** refrained from laying **out in toys and** confectionery the simple earnings gained when other children of his age were enjoying sports that his active young spirits longed to engage in.

" Here are two oranges, mother. Only think, a gentleman gave them to me of his own ac- **cord! I s'pose,** though, he saw me looking at 'em pretty hard," cried James, bursting in

one day, and giving, with a blush, the last clause
of his story in a less firm tone than the two
preceding. But as the owner of the kind eyes
looking so lovingly into his could not find it
in her heart to chide him, he continued, ex-
citedly, —

'Please, cut 'em into seven pieces, and save
one for father."

"Yes, save the biggest for father. Mayn't
she, Jimmy?" shouted the little girls, following Marion to the closet for a plate and knife,
and patiently awaiting their share of the lus-
cious fruit.

"Father" was always remembered. The
gentle teachings of the wronged wife were never
against one whose strong arms should have
sheltered, where, instead, they enfeebled.

Soon Harvard found his pea-nut business less
lucrative than at first. Other boys, seeing how
well he was doing, engaged in it. To his surprise, they sold more for the same money than

he was able to. He did not know how they could do this, until he caught two of them filling their pockets from the boxes of a grocer, who was waiting on customers. This disclosure troubled Harvard. As he was the only one who knew of the theft, he felt it to be his imperative duty to inform the grocer. Yet, although feeling that the boys were guilty, his kind heart trembled for them, and very likely apprehended a harsher punishment than they would receive. He concluded, after some deliberation in the store, to confer with his mother before saying anything to the grocer. As if to help him out of his difficulty, and just as he was going to advise the boys to make confession to the grocer, — which plan his mother had proposed, — they were detected in a repetition of the theft.

Previous to their detection, however, they met Harvard as he was stopping to sell his honest merchandise to a group of school-children.

"Don't buy of him! He is real mean! We will sell you more," shouted the dealers of ill-gotten pea-nuts, rushing up and pressing Harvard into the background.

"I'll patronize you, boys," answered a hand-somely-dressed lad, very pompous and impor-tant, eyeing with ineffable scorn our downcast hero.

"Oh, Fred Uhland! Aren't you ashamed to buy of those mean boys who shoved that boy, behind there, right out of his place?" cried a voice, sweet-toned and clear, that made Harvard's heart leap and his cheek flush.

"No; I don't forget some things," was his dogged reply. Fred knew Harvard at a glance.

"Here, little fellow, how much do you ask for the whole of your pea-nuts?" asked the same very sweet voice.

"Thirty cents," replied Harvard, without raising his eyes, — a fierce struggle the while going on in his breast.

"Only thirty cents? How lucky for me! I've got just the sum." And tiny white fingers dropped bits of silver into Harvard's palm, while the musical voice counted the amount.

"Now, boys and girls, help yourselves. I couldn't eat so many in a year!"

As Aurora spoke, she held the basket, while her school-mates gathered about her. Fred Uhland, who had purchased a quart of nuts of the dishonest boys, stood aloof, sulkily and meanly keeping his to himself, yet wishing for a handful out of his cousin's basket. When Aurora returned the basket to Harvard, his grateful eyes would meet hers.

"Why, it is you! How is your head? You can't think how much I thought of it after I left you," said Aurora, interestedly.

"Better, I thank you; quite well, long ago," softly answered Harvard, turning aside his face, too full to utter another word; too con scious to trust himself near her long. Yet his grateful remembrance bade him ask, —

"Is Miss Horne well?"

"Miss Horne? Who is she? I think I don't know her," replied Aurora, pondering over the name.

"I mean Sally; you remember the girl who brought you down to see me that day when — "

"Oh, Sally! But I never heard her called Miss before. She is quite well. I think I'll tell her how politely and properly you inquired for her. 'Miss Horne' sounds very nice and respectable," said Aurora.

Harvard laughed with her, not that he meant by so doing to cast the slightest reflection upon the claims of Sally to respectful mention, but simply because Aurora's mirth was very contagious.

"Miss Horne often speaks of you. But isn't it funny? she won't tell me what your name is, nor will the others. You will? — there's a good boy."

Poor Harvard was sorely tried. She was a charming coaxer. He did not wish to give her pain. By determined importunity on Aurora's part, and fearing unpleasant results if he refused her after all this, he gave her the desired information.

" Why! and you once owned my pretty pony! I do wish I could give it back to you. I shall never enjoy riding as I have. Oh dear, dear, what a queer world! And you once lived in my beautiful home, and admired it, oh, so much! I know you couldn't help doing so. And now you are not rich. I may not be always. Oh dear, dear, how strange everything is!" cried Aurora.

" I did not want to tell you my name. You saw that. But now that you know it, I will just say that you must never believe one unkind thing about my mother. She is the best mother in the whole world."

" I dare say she is, for you are such a nice boy. I am really sorry I said she was different from that. I never will again."

" Aurora, Aurora!" cried her impatient companions, who stood wondering near.

" If you don't leave that low boy this minute, I'll tell your parents!" cried Fred Uhland.

" I must go, Harvard. I am not afraid of Fred's threat, though, I want you to understand. I must go. Good-bye." A new phase of life had opened to Aurora.

" Please don't forget to tell Miss Horne that I often think of her, and shall never forget her kindness to me," cried Harvard.

" I will be sure to do so. Oh dear, I wish you were rich! I don't want anybody to be poor. I wish I could make you rich."

Aurora did not see in the sparkling eye, erect bearing, and animated manner, how rich she had made Harvard, who thought not of poverty nor wrong while with her. He would not have exchanged that small space of sidewalk, so occupied, for Victoria's throne. So much joy comes from friendly, appreciative recognition! And here the boy and girl separated. She had seen him, and was not ashamed to own him for an acquaintance. That delicious truth was joy to him for many succeeding days, even when poverty came nearer, and with cruel pinches showed him the folly of dreaming dreams the most seemingly unreal and unsubstantial that ever infested a human brain.

"I will be a man some day, and carry my family up to the hight from which it was hurled by more than one evil spirit," had been his resolve during the never-forgotten visit at the mansion of Mr. Umber. This purpose was no unsubstantial offspring of a miserable day.

"Lina tells me you mean to aspire high,"

said Dariel, during a conversation with Harvard at the home of the former.

" Yes, sir," simply replied the boy, dropping his eyes, for Dariel's still fine eyes seemed to be reading him through to his very soul.

" How high ? " softly asked the old man.

" As high as I can. I mean to be rich, brave, learned, generous, and good," replied Harvard with kindling eye.

" What do you mean by good ? That goodness which springs from the Maker of all goodness ? "

" Yes," murmured Harvard.

" Then it will be well with thee, my son. I am glad you have come to me to-day. I am glad that Abel Lumbkin took me in his easy chaise down to see Lina yesterday. For the sweet girl and I are bound on the same long journey. We start soon. I may never see you again, for I feel that my days are numbered. But I want you to promise me — more, to promise Heaven — ever to work for Christ's kingdom. Lina's efforts have been most glorious in the work. You have her example to work by. Keep not your light hidden. ' Whosoever, therefore, shall confess me before men, him will I confess before my Father which is in heaven.' "

" I want to work for Christ. But sometimes, when I speak of him and his merciful love, I get laughed at. Boys generally hate to hear such tidings."

" True, Harvy. Still, though often discouraged, you must labor on. You must creep before you walk. You must confess Christ before all men. You will meet inconsistencies and imperfections and scoffers, even among children, but such discoveries must not lessen your efforts to swell the King's army. Let all your acts declare, ' Christ is my Master, and I am Christ's disciple.' "

Harvard listened attentively, and when the good old man paused, almost breathless and overcome, the boy felt that never again in this life would they meet.

When Harvy next saw Dariel, the pleasant eye was closed; the true lips silenced; the faithful heart quiet, never to be wounded by friend or foe again. Warren and Marion attended the funeral, and memory softened the heart of the former to the shedding of bitter tears.

"I knew I should never meet on earth the good old man again," said Lina, with an angelic smile, "but I shall join him soon."

CHAPTER XI.

" She enjoys sweet peace for evermore,
    As weather-beaten ships arrived on happy shore."

LINA'S disease now assumed a more gloomy form. Nothing, not even her favorite nephew's fervent prayers, could save her. He saw this, and his bosom heaved with dread. The little children in the neighborhood, who loved to look upon her sweet face as she sat working at the window whenever her strength permitted, whispered to each other, but took care not to let her see that they had noticed anything unusual in her appearance. Even the most noisy little feet and most boisterous of juvenile voices were mysteriously subdued as they neared the house wherein she breathed

12   177

the hours away. Again, her door would be cautiously opened, and a bunch of flowers or wreath of forest leaves held forth for her acceptance; sometimes an orange, nice cake, or apple, in like manner would be presented. At such times Lina would beckon with a thin, waxen hand for the little donor to approach her chair or couch, when she would say something so very sweet by way of thanks, and, besides, drop some priceless pearl from Bibledepths into the young, susceptible heart, that it was made the richer for its deed of kindness and love.

But who can describe the pain of seeing all this going on? Harvard's strength nearly gave out. He had left school to attend on Lina in the precious moments left her. He knew they were very few. And yet he could scarcely bring his mind to believe the greatness of the anticipated evil. Daily and hourly he strove to read in Lina's serene face a different story;

daily and hourly the warning finger of the destroyer bade the boy read many a sad, sad mark aright.

And for this early summons Lina felt no regret, as far as self was concerned. For years she had seemed like one scarce of the earth. Gentle deeds, patient submission, angel-ministrations, forgetfulness of self, had been natural to her. Yet, ah! the weary days of her blighted youth! Sometimes memory would linger with torturing tenacity over the sunny hours of infancy. Then hope and patience would be entreated to stay and light up the solemn present with their radiant smiles until the future should be reached,—a glorious future! And now she felt with inexpressible joy that that longed-for future was waiting very near,—a mere mist between.

"Oh, how can you?" sobbed Harvard, when, at the close of an exceedingly sick day, Lina lay smiling, happy with thoughts of that near Eden home.

> " ' The Father of eternal light
>   Shall there his beams display,
> And not one moment's darkness mix
>   With that unvaried day,' "

replied Lina. " Harvard," she continued, " there will be no shadows there. Think of it! All trials and sorrows gone! Ever abiding love and peace!" She paused a moment, her face still radiant and triumphant. Then she added, in a lower tone, so gentle and persuasive, — " And you, — how will it be with you, Harvard? We have been close together *here*, Harvy."

" And will be *there*," sobbed the boy.

" The other children, too, Harvy. They look up to you," continued Lina.

" I will try to do for them what you would have done for me, Lina. But how can I, and you gone? "

Marion had overhead this, and saw the hand o: Lina seek Harvard's by way of comfort, and of showing grateful approval of his promise. She left her work and sat beside the cot, when her mind ran swiftly over the years between her wedding day and this. What was she then, — on her bridal morn? What was Lina?

"'And if I go and prepare a place for you, I will come again and receive you unto myself, that where I am, there ye may be also,'" whispered Lina, who had quickly interpreted the mental condition of her sister.

These were sweet words, yet they came with a mingling of pain and pleasure. The present held little enough of joy for Marion; often she felt herself very near the portal through which Lina would soon pass. But there were her children! Lina whispered, —

"Marion, if possible, keep Harvard at school a few years longer. He can earn something when out of school. Sell my bracelet and

chain, and my beautiful Bessie ; it will be less
trouble than to let her.   These sales will bring
you in something to defray the expenses of
keeping him at school ; his clothes he can obtain himself; his books and tuition are free.
Oh, what a chance that — tuition and books
free — for an ambitious boy ! "

Marion leaned over and kissed the wan, dear
face, upon which her tears fell.

" Sister, don't cry for me.   If you could realize my happiness !   It is as if the gates of
heaven were opening ! "

" You have been upon the threshold all your
days, Lina ! "

" Hardly, Marion.   My feet were prone to
wander stubbornly away."

A few moments after, Lina spoke again : —

" Sister, I must finish what I had begun, and
don't let it make you weep.   Keep of my clothing whatever will be useful for Grace and Margie.   The rest, those rich silk and muslin frocks

that I outgrew long ago, and couldn't bear to part with because mamma bought and made them for me, — dispose of them to dealers in second-hand clothing; that will help defray the expenses of my — of my — "

Here Lina was interrupted by irrepressible sobs. Harvard came round from the side of the cot where he had been sitting, and threw himself in helpless grief upon his mother's bosom, crying as he did so, — "Oh, mamma, mamma, we can't spare Lina!"

That wail was heard by Mr. Hoyt, who came home sober and pleasant. Lina motioned for him to approach her. With instinctive delicacy Marion and Harvard left them together. Whatever Lina's parting words to Warren were, he never revealed them. He left her, and with a grave face sought slumber. If anything like remorse visited his pillow that sad night, it did him and his family little good; for, alas! he was too closely in the toils of the tempter, and lacked a genuine desire to be set free.

Mrs. Lumbkin, whose occasional incipient resentment against Mr. Hoyt for slighting her husband had ever vanished before her sympathy, now came in to watch and assist as she might be needed; but Marion and Harvard did not leave Lina, who said, while holding forth her hand to the kind woman, —

" I am glad you are here. *They* will need your help before long for me. Do not weep. I can not talk if you do. I want you to be sure how happy Christ's children are when near their dying hour. Oh, how I love Him ! And how I want you, dear Mrs. Lumbkin, to tell Christ's love everywhere ! Will you ? "

" I will. Who could help giving you that answer, child ? Who, truly loving Christ, can help bidding sinners seek him ? "

" But do you mean it ? He is listening to you. What you may say only to comfort me will not make the salvation of the erring sure, dear friend."

" I do mean it. I will attend to the welfare of every soul within my reach and means."

" That will do. He has heard it. He is close by," said Lina. " Oh that I had done more for Him ! "

The little girls were next brought in for her to kiss and bid good-night. They clung around her and then departed, too young to have perceived anything uncommon in her parting embrace.

" How pretty they are, Marion ! I used to hope I might live to see them grown up. But how much better to hope to meet them again, and be no more separated for ever ! " said Lina, when Mrs. Lumbkin had taken them away.

" Is that Jimmy creeping about the foot of the bed ? " asked the dying one, mindful of everything.

" Yes, Lina," said Jimmy, wiping away his

tears with the back of his hand, and essaying a manly front.

" Come ! "

Jimmy needed no second bidding. Ready were his tears and promises as Lina clasped her arms around him and whispered in his ear. And now Jimmy is taken from the room, understanding to the full what was near at hand, almost seeing the shade mounting, never to be removed on earth.

Slowly the truth that Lina is dying is received by Harvard. He questions it, with streaming eyes.

" How can it be, when she lies smiling and speaking words of comfort and affection ? ' He cometh like a thief in the night,' " suddenly remembered Harvard, who as suddenly implored, — " But not to our door ! Oh, no ; not here, where all is serene and fair and untroubled ! "

But *there*, across *that* threshold, the death-angel came.

When Aurora had lighted the eastern skies with inimitable hues, Lina lay white and still and cold!

When the other children awoke, and learned what had happened, they entreated Harvard to take them out of doors.

" Go to my house and eat breakfast, children. And, Harvard, tell Tony to ask Mrs. Lyle to come here as soon as she can," said Mrs. Lumbkin, whose eyes were red and swollen.

" I know what she wants Mrs. Lyle for. She makes such long, dreadful white dresses! Leo has shown them to me. How can Mrs. Lyle feel like making them!" thought Jimmy.

The children went through the form of taking breakfast at Mrs. Lumbkin's. Abel and his sons were hospitable and kind.

" Let us walk out, Harvard. I feel as if I were stifling," whispered Jimmy.

As the children stood on the sidewalk, list-less, aching, and restless, a wagon rattled along the street, then turned down their court. It had something low and long covered up in the bottom. Harvard turned away his eyes, and led the little girls out of sight. But Jimmy stopped to see where the wagon was going, wondering what it was bringing. The wagon stopped at his door; the cloth was removed from the mysterious something. The sight thus revealed was too much for Jimmy; he fell helpless to the ground.

"Oh, Harvy, Harvy, it's for her! it's for her!"

"What's the matter, my boy?"

Jimmy raised his head, and beheld his in-terlocutor, an oldish, queer-looking man, gaz-ing pityingly upon him.

"I'm 'most dead! And that's for her,— Lina!"

"Lina?"

" Lina Mayburn, my mother's sister."

The gentleman frowned, looked down the court, and saw the burden the men were carrying through a battered doorway.

" Is she dead ? " he asked, in a sorrowful whisper.

" She died this morning. I wish we were all dead! It's awful to live here ! "

" How is your mother ? "

" Almost dead. We're all almost dead ! "

" Poor child ! " And the gentleman drew forth his purse. " Here, give this to her. I used to know her. She was a beautiful girl, and as good as beautiful. And Lina, — what a lovely pet she was ! There, my boy, run in with that. There's no knowing what we may come to. But what would my wife say if she knew of my doing this ! Don't mention this to her ! "

" I can't ; I don't know her."

" No, you don't, and are not likely to ; that's

the worst of it. She ought to be there — in that old house — with her cousin, your mother, or rather in a better one. But what am I saying! Run home, and give my love and sympathy to your mother."

"Who shall I tell her you are?" asked Jimmy.

"Nobody."

While Jimmy stood gazing after the singular man, Harvard retraced his steps, and thus came upon one who, scoffed at at home, often abroad showed he possessed a heart capable of fine, strong feeling. Harvard was in no danger of not recognizing Mr. Umber. A never-forgotten day had impressed his countenance, with certain others, upon his memory.

"And you're another of them, I warrant! And those little girls too, I dare say," cried Mr. Umber, with a sudden halt.

"Our surname is Hoyt. Did you mean that?" said Harvard.

" Yes, 1 did. There's no knowing what we may come to. You ought to be better clad. I hope your mother will not think I keep my wife away from her. I'd scorn to do it."

" No, sir; she will never think such a thing of you. Indeed, she will not, Mr. Umber."

" What! Do you know my name? Ah, now I remember; you came to my house with your father. I shan't forget that occasion. But you used to come with both your parents when you were a baby, and all be made enough of. You don't remember that, though. You have a better look than my boy. Shouldn't wonder if you make a better man. Good-bye."

The money contained in the purse was more than sufficient to pay the expenses of Lina's funeral. So the pretty dresses she had mentioned were left in the little trunk packed by fingers now cold and stiff. Marion did not even lift the lid, but her .tears fell plentifully upon it. Bessie found a ready purchaser in the man

who had let her for her board so long. She
did not bring a high price, for she had seen her
best days, though still useful enough to be
profitable. Lina had never mounted her since
that last ride with Harvard, when Jetty became
the property of Aurora White, through his
father's loss at cards a few evenings before.

Mr. Umber was not the only friend the Hoyt
family found at this period. Mrs. Moreland
sent Marion a full suit of black, and ten dollars besides. This lady was in ill-health, and
went south soon after her welcome gift reached
Marion. Mrs. Torrey added to these favors a
comfortable suit of clothes for each of the children; she sent them anonymously, fearing
Marion would reject the package if she knew
its source. All this thoughtfulness showed that
she had not a heart quite after the model of
her husband's.

"If I could only have an opportunity to
place a marble slab over her grave! But that

day will never come, I fear," Marion often
sighed. But one Sabbath afternoon she was
much surprised to find a grave-stone of pure
white marble, upon which was inscribed,
" AND A LITTLE CHILD SHALL LEAD THEM,"
just where she had hoped to be able to place
one. She wondered with tears who could have
performed so kind an act. She was sure none
of her haughty relatives had been so thoughtful. She never knew. But Abel and Dolly
did. They had lovingly erected the stone
themselves. Near by rested the dreamless
form of old Dariel; at his head also they had
placed a modest stone, thereon written, —
" WELL DONE, GOOD AND FAITHFUL SERVANT!"

13

CHAPTER XII.

" Eager to hope, but not less firm to bear,
  Acquainted with all feelings save despair."

THREE years of grave experience had passed since Lina died. No waste spot was her little grave. In summer the flowers she loved bloomed above it; and in winter small footprints marked a pathway to the snow-hidden mound. Harvard was now thirteen years old, and very small and thin. His face had lost nothing of its spiritual beauty, nor had his soul. The boy had striven earnestly for the good of all about him, but mourned deeply and in secret over the waste spot in his father's heart which he feared would never be reclaimed; yet, though thus fearing, never withholding effort, encouragement, and assistance. His mother, though in better health, was more despondent. The family now occupied poorer rooms than ever; furnished rooms, too, and of the meanest description. Mrs. Lyle lived near. Between her son **Leo** and Harvy there existed a firm friendship. Both were upright, aspiring, and earnest little fellows; both struggling toward light through exceeding gloom. The glimpse of light that Harvy felt so grateful for, as it peered above his former home, had grown very small, for close high walls and towering chimneys shut it nearly out of sight.

Still, though missing every familiar object, the furniture and simple appointments of his preceding home among the rest, his hopeful eye saw beauties even in his new abode, not the least of which was, that quite near were wharves and ships, and thronged offices and stores in towering buildings devoted to merchandise.

Here was busy life, and Harvard was glad to behold it.

Business always gave his young blood a thrill of delight. In this part of the city Harvard found profitable jobs. The money he now earned he was in the habit of slipping into his mother's pocket unseen by all save herself. There was need of this, for Mr. Hoyt had grown exacting, unscrupulous, and indifferent to everything but his vile needs. And about those wharves Harvard often obtained employment for his mother's needle, and, we may add, for her hands at other work. Warren Hoyt little knew the means by which Marion, with the aid of her children, managed to keep the family from asking alms, or seeking a residence among common paupers.

"It seems to me, mother, as if I could do something more toward helping you along. I propose to leave school and study as I find time. Although they do their best at earning and sav-

ing, the children are greatly in need of necessary things," said Harvard, one evening, after a
thoughtful silence.

"But you are so young, Harry, and now
looking dreadfully overworked! I wish I could
give you rest. You are too young, my son, to
work harder than you do."

"Never mind about my youth. Why, when
I hear most boys of my age talk, and see them
act, it seems as if I were three times as old as
they," cried Harvard, without a shadow of ego-
tism, raising his kindling face, and unconsciously stretching his slight figure to its utmost
hight.

"In spirit you are almost a man, my son,"
said the other in a brighter tone, willing to let
him cherish a hope she had long ago given up,
—a hope for better days, for the good time
coming, that youth and unbroken spirits are
constantly expecting.

"In size, too, or shall be soon, I dare say,"

added Harvard, gayly, yet casting a dissatisfied eye at his very small hand and **arm,**— little strength in **either,** though great willingness and activity.

" **You will very** likely be as tall **as your** father, **Harvy,"** said Marion, speaking in a sighing **way, which** disappointed people are apt to acquire.

" But not like him in anything else, I know. Good-evening, folks," interrupted a hitherto unperceived listener, advancing toward the scanty fire where the others sat.

" **My** husband was once worthy to be the example **of** any man," replied Marion in a tone of gentle reproof, while a flush expressive **of** injured feeling **rushed to her thin** cheek.

" How came **you in here, without** our knowing it till **now?"** demanded Harvard, who thought the **woman not entitled to respect,** because of her **unkind and** unexpected interference.

" I did not creep in, young man. I lifted the latch and walked in with my usual noise, which you would have heard if you had not been so busy talking and thinking; bright employments, both, I dare say."

Harvard could see by the firelight the sneer on the speaker's face. His blood burned at the sight, and the old wish of long ago — that he were a man — rose at once. But he did not understand her.

" You are rude and insulting," he cried, with rapidly filling eyes.

" My son ! " implored his mother.

" It's of no use to coax me, mother."

" That's truth ; you are made of as stern stuff as iron. I've always seen that, especially when you've been doing all sorts of jobs. — taking care of the children, helping your poor mother even on her sewing, talking like a man with your father, and getting your lessons, all at once, so it seems to me. I said poor mo-

ther, a moment ago : I ought to have said rich
mother; she is so, with such a son."

Harvard's face relaxed a little, but yet indi-
cated a deal of astonishment, as he saw Mrs.
Humphrey composedly seating herself behind
Mrs. Hoyt upon the high-backed wooden settle,
and beginning to knit with great energy and
coolness.

"Now, young man, I expect you are mighty
angry with me ; but I don't care if you are.   I
have seen madder folks in my day, and been
worse in that way myself — "

"Mother," interposed Harvard, "how can
you bear this talk?   What a strange woman
she must be !"

"Hush, Harvy."

"I've tried to keep still, mother.   But don't
she try your feelings?   She does mine."

"Wait a moment, boy, and then I'll go.   I
came in for your good.   I don't want to stay
where I'm not wanted, — not I.   But I never

had the way of getting on well with people **at first.** I mean well, all the time, though," replied Mrs. Humphrey, knitting awhile quietly, and thus making her moment a long one **to** our impatient **hero,** who sat deprecating her presence and interference, or wondering why his mother came to be so superior to her sex. At length Mrs. Humphrey resumed, —

" **My** paper — now listen, Harvard — tells of a heap of **wants, until I** began to think there was nothing but wants in the world, except people longing and waiting for places ;"—Harvard gave a dismal groan here ;—" but at length I found, sure, that I was mistaken, for I saw a chance — "

" **What** was it ? " cried Harvard, springing to his feet and reaching his cap from its peg.

" A place for a lad to learn the shoemaker's trade, — board, clothes, evening-schooling, and **fifty** dollars a year, for three years, though if a boy is smart the boss usually raises the salary every year, I've heard. To be sure, you might find something better,—more genteel. My errand's done. There!"

Mrs. Humphrey's listener's hopes drooped as she repeated the words of the advertisement. Harvy dropped back upon his seat. But pride has many a thrust in its course through the world. None knew that truth better than Harvard and his mother. Harvard sat silent a moment. More than one tear was forced back, and many a sob subdued, by the fear that he was ungrateful and selfish, or worse, perhaps, —aspiring after things of earth, earthly.

"I thank you," at length came heartily, while his face, if pale, looked full of gratitude, then flushed at the remembrance of rudeness and incivility.

" Well, I'll take the ' thank you,' but not the blush on your open face that seems to want to apologize for your high words to me; for my own way, as I have said, is none of the smoothest and pleasantest. I'm always ruffling people up when I don't want to, for people find it hard to understand me. Good-night."

And Mrs. Humphrey was going as suddenly as she came, when Harvard seized her hand, and whispered,—

"Forgive me! I can not sleep unless you do!"

"I do, and hope you'll forgive me."

As she spoke, her tones were low and gentle; but her hearers could not see how full of un-shed tears were her eyes, nor how full of a desire to help was her heart. Indeed, a desire to assist the Hoyt family had for some time pressed painfully upon her. She deprecated her poverty as never before, and with a heavy spirit was about going to her own poor room, when she was again intercepted, and by Jimmy, who, running to the closet, brought from thence an apple, the only one he had, which he thrust into her l and, without saying a single word.

Mrs. Humphrey caught Jimmy as he was bashfully retreating, and kissed his broad forehead.

"I never met such a family before. The Lord be good to 'em!" she murmured, wiping her eyes, and leaving the room.

"What do you say to this opportunity?" asked Mrs. Hoyt, when the door had closed upon their neighbor.

"I think Mrs. Humphrey very good to mention it. But—but—"

"But what?" asked the mother, kindly, although her own bosom held the answer.

"I did hope, or rather used to, that I should get something better to do; something that our kindred—the buried ones, I mean—would not think mean. They were used to such different things."

Mrs. Hoyt's bosom throbbed with joy at finding her son had no fear of the disapprobation of the purse-proud relatives who stood aloof in her fallen fortunes. It was a mastery over self that she had not wholly gained.

"What trade had you rather learn?" she asked, hesitatingly, **for** she hated to break in upon the revery **into** which Harvard had fallen.

"A printer's."

"Is it not **fully as** laborious as that of shoemaker?"

"Possibly. But **you see, mother,** it gives **a** fellow a better chance."

"How?"

"Oh, he can **go on with** his studies,— that is if he cares to. Chances for that are all around him. You know he can't help gaining a great deal of knowledge, and can just as easily turn it to advantage if he cares to. I was in a printing-office last week to see if I could get any work to do there, and such heaps of books and papers as I saw!" And Harvard stopped, fairly choking with sighs and tears.

"**My** poor child! What will become of him

if he has to go on in this way? Oh, Warren, Warren, could your eyes but be opened to see the blight you have brought upon your family!" thought Mrs. Hoyt.

"I hope you won't think anything of my nonsense, mother," observed Harvard, upon suddenly meeting her pitying gaze. "I don't get down very often, you know."

And he smiled as he spoke, and thought his voice very calm and even. Poor little Harvard! his soul spoke in every lineament and syllable.

"Perhaps you can obtain a situation in a printing-office," said Mrs. Hoyt, casting about in her mind the possibility of the thing.

"At any rate I can see, mother. If I can't, why, I'll try the other. You know if I learn the trade I may not always be obliged to work at it. Great and good men have come from the shoemaker's bench. My objection to it was, that I could not make as much money and get as much knowledge there as I might in some other situation," returned Harvard, with the happy changefulness of childhood, and the ready adaptation that characterizes the same brief period.

This change in **Harvard** so cheered Jimmy that he declared himself tired enough to go to bed and sleep all night.

After this, Harvard **took from** his book-shelf a favorite history, the **Life** of Franklin, from which he read aloud **to his** mother, **who, with** senses seemingly locked up in the exercise, was wondering in deep anguish what the future had in store **for** her little ones. So has many **a** mother in similar circumstances wondered, — wondered. When, oh! when will the maternal heart cease agonizing over intemperance ? There are household scenes and trials of every shape; there are accidents and circumstances which we call visitations; and all that we can say of their result is, that it is the divine will.

They come as the twilight shadows that troop along the wall. God grant that whenever the unsought-for chalice is pressed to our lips, we shall always make the same response. But there are sorrows that press hard and near by, — sorrows that are not of God's appointment.

Who will sit idle and see these sorrows, not God-appointed, thronging up, when every breath we draw is an immense power in itself, — a power crowded with will, might, and strength? Truly, if we let our hands fall at our side, and our tongue remain dumb, we are but as dry vines that cumber the ground. God help us, then, in that time when he shall demand of us what we have done with our talents!

Harvard read on, but this evening was not destined to be free from unpleasant interruptions. At nine o'clock his father came staggering in, and, with some startling incoherencies of speech, tumbled upon the bed in a

corner of the **room, and fell into a deep slum-**
ber.

Harvard, who had paused at the interruption,
could not resume his reading; this was too
rough a realization of facts. With compressed
lips and burning checks he watched the brutal
form of that parent who should have been his
guide and shield.

" Mother," he cried, " mother, is it right that
we should suffer so ? "

" My son, my son ! in whose hands are all
the corners of the earth?" **was asked with**
quivering lip.

"**Ah, but** He sees this," pointing wildly to
the corner where lay the inebriate, " and lets
it be ! "

"**My** child ! **my child !** you frighten me ; "
and tenderly the poor mother laid her hands
on that dear young head, **and besought faith**
and trust to abide in her humble home.

" Faith and **trust**," repeated Harvard in in-

14

ward penitence and remorse. "Would that they could end the storms that tire my heart!" and he joined his mother in every desire expressed in her fervent prayer.

"Mother, I feel well now," he said, after a thoughtful silence, "and will henceforth try to keep down bad thoughts. How selfish in me to break out in your presence, if I must break out somewhere! I will try to be better."

"My noble boy!" she said, with a gush of maternal tenderness.

They had separated for the night, when Harvard descended the attic-stairs, and, opening the door a crack, said, —

"Mother, do you feel quite easy about me?"

"I do, my son."

"Not a single bad feeling left in your heart, mother?"

"None of your placing there, darling."

"Do you think Mrs. Humphrey has quite

forgiven me? I was so rude and ready to take offense!"

"Do not let a single fear disturb you, my love. She has too good a heart to cherish unkind feelings, especially when she saw the reason you had for being moved. I think, Harvy, we have all more pride than we are comfortable with; and I far more than you."

"Don't find any fault with yourself, mother. I can't bear that. You are all that is good and perfect; the best mother boy ever had!"

"My darling flatterer!"

"Not good enough yet to be that, mother. Not good enough yet to be anything." With this, Harvard slipped off the stair, and stood quivering with emotion before the pale, weary woman, still plying her needle by the light of a poor lamp.

"What is it, child?"

"Dearest, most patient mother, have you, oh, have you forgotten and forgiven that out burst against — against — " he began timidly, flushing all over with pain and sorrow and awe.

" Have I forgotten it ? Have I forgiven it ? Oh, child, when did you ever wound me of yourself ? Only be careful not to lose for one moment your confidence in Heaven ! Lose that, and you will indeed suffer. He does see and permit many things. But it is not for the finite mind to question why. Nor are we to mete out our measures of temporal good or evil. We, my child, are to keep ourselves as far as possible ' pure and unspotted from the world.' Can not we do this pretty well ? If we but array ourselves in the imperishable armor of the Christian, and stand on our guard, can not we ? "

" Yes, mother, if we will always remember."

But how wistful Harvard's face looked, as it rested on his mother's bosom. And how clearly she read in his tearful eye, " How can I always

keep ' pure and unspotted from the world ' ? "
So she repeated, in soothing tones, —

" ' I love them that love me.' ' He that
is of God heareth God's word.' ' I will lift up
mine eyes unto the hills, from whence cometh
my help.' ' A little that a righteous man hath
is better than the riches of the wicked.' ' Come
unto me, all ye that are weary and heavy-
laden.' "

Harvard did not answer; his tongue seemed
to cleave to the roof of his mouth. But the
eyes of both mother and child were swimming.
Their hearts were very full. Moments flew by
on golden pinions, — moments of great present
joy and rich promise, never forgotten by either.

Harvard had scarcely re-entered his chamber
ere the door of one opposite was opened, and
Mrs. Humphrey stepped across the entry. A
low voice in prayer arrested her as she was
about to lift the latch of Harvard's door.

" Keep my spirit full of Thy love. I can not

be good one moment if I forget thy presence and mercy. Make me patient with my poor father, considerate of my dear mother, thoughtful of the children, and careful to wound nobody's feelings. O my Heavenly Father, I do not think I can keep myself ' pure and unspotted from the world,' unless thou wilt stoop to abide with me continually, even with me; and I know that thou wilt humble thyself to do so, unless I permit ever waiting sin to lead me into darkness," pleaded Harvard's voice, broken and tearful.

When he had ceased, Mrs. Humphrey gently knocked at the door.

When the boy answered the summons, Mrs. Humphrey said, —

" What I want to mention is, that if you take *your* words to heart, I shall *mine,* and let 'em worry me to death! My roughness, when I meant only kindness, made you speak as you did."

" You are too good," replied Harvard, reaching forth his hand, which was warmly taken by Mrs. Humphrey.

This episode made the two firm friends ever after; any little abruptness of manner, or seemingly uncalled-for hauteur, or exhibition of temper on either side, could never again produce uncomfortable feelings.

" I'll give you the paper containing the ' want,' " said Mrs. Humphrey at the conclusion of this interview.

" I shall be glad of it," replied Harvard, who added, when the door was closed upon her, " I must control my temper, be less proud, and try to understand people. She is a real good woman, but has queer ways that are aggravating to one of my temper. Yet, just because I did not understand her, I was rude to her. I must be polite and kind, and study people in order to treat them fairly."

CHAPTER XIII.

"A man hath the tiller in his hand, and may steer against the cur-
    rent,
  Or may glide down idle with the stream, till his vessel founder in
    the whirlpool."

"WELL, mother," said Harvard cheerfully the next morning, "I think I'll try for a situation to-day. This city'll surely give me a chance."

"Shall you try the printing-offices first?"

"Yes; and the counting-rooms and stores."

"The last won't pay you much, Harvy; mostly nothing; for I inquired last week. I wanted a chance myself," interposed Jimmy, as he snapped a whip, — a present from a team- ster who liked the boy's looks.

"At present they would not pay a great deal,

216

I suppose; but after a while they do well for a fellow who works hard," replied Harvard, amused at the unsuspected effort of Jimmy to get such business.

"I'm willing to work hard, but nobody'll give me anything to do. Here's mother wearing herself out, and has had to sell everything but herself and us. It is too bad. One man told me to 'go home and let my mother rock me to sleep.' Now wasn't that saucy? He asked my name, and then called me a bold, ambitious baby. I didn't mean to, but I burst out crying right there. That made the man laugh; I guess he likes to make children feel badly. I remembered that man's looks, and last Saturday he happened to pass me as I was helping Tony Lumbkin carry letters, and Tony told me the man was named Torrey. He is rich and a lawyer; and — but what makes you so pale, mother?"

Marion thought of two splendid estates in

the suburbs of the city that this man Torrey had helped wrest from her family.

Harvard had a dim recollection of this man. He did not say so, for it was a memory of woe.

" Little brother, at present do not try to get different business from that you have. After a while something bright will turn up for you," he said.

" How would a peep into law-offices do, mother?" he added, turning to the matron presiding with grace and dignity at a very simple table.

" You can see. You seem to have thought of everything, my son."

" Except going to sea."

" Of course you will not do that."

" Never fear, mother; I have no fancy that way. If I had, I would not leave you, as you are situated, for it."

Mrs. Hoyt looked her gratitude.

"I have thought of everything, mother. I hardly slept last night for thinking."

" But you needed sleep, child."

" I did not feel the loss of it. My mind was in a happy state. It seemed as if anywhere in the whole world I could find friends in plenty. I went to bed, but soon rose and dressed myself, and sat at the window. Oh, mother! how like a thousand loving eyes the stars looked down at me!"

"'The heavens declare thy glory, Lord ; the firmament showeth thy handiwork,'" said the sweet tones of the sympathizing mother.

"They do, they do, mother! And as they thus looked, I felt as if I could do anything, I seemed so strong. This morning I shall set out in good earnest. See if I don't do something to-day, mother!"

" I am confident you will. Shall you answer the advertisement?"

" If I can do no better."

Mrs. Hoyt ate in silence, occasionally glancing at the bright face of Harvard. Not for worlds would she have dispelled a single hope that animated him, nor would she, as she valued her peace, have derided a glimmer of a trust that beckoned on, and upheld him in fresh trials. But she could not avoid contrasting her situation now with that she enjoyed at his birth, when all that fortune could give was lavished upon her,—when the past had been a pleasant dream, and the future promised bounteously.

She felt with a secret pang that her noble child had a conflict before him that none of his ancestors had been driven to engage in ; a conflict hard enough to make a stout heart quail, for poverty is as relentless as powerful.

"I am ready, mother," said Harvard, having finished his breakfast, combed his hair, blacked his boots, and brushed his well-worn clothes. As he spoke he looked wistfully up at her.

She laid her hand upon his head. "May your noble efforts meet the success they deserve! And thou, O Father! wilt thou bless and gladden his way as only thou canst!" were the words of that full loving heart, and then Marion's true lips were affectionately pressed upon her child's forehead.

With a bright eye and cheerful air the little adventurer passes from her presence, a basket of pea-nuts suspended from his arm, for he could not neglect an opportunity of adding to the family income. A pair of humid eyes follow his progress down the street, while the same watcher prays that blessings deep and full may crown to overflowing that young unselfish life.

His walk was delightful; even that part of it, with its sad sights and bad air, that of necessity belonged to the district in which he lived, could not overshadow his spirits.

The day was fine, a glorious commencement of October, with a clear healthful breeze redolent of harvest perfume. The sky was veiled with hazy clouds. The nearer trees, together with those more distant, and the verdure crowning a far-off line of hills, were gorgeous with red, purple, russet, and gold, in all the shades that artist-pencil delights to portray. The soil was crisp, and had a pleasant spring for the feet, as it seemed to our hero, who had to pass the costly mansion of Mr. Torrey. Harvard remembered its erection, and a conversation he held with his mother in reference to its beauty. He stifled his sigh and went on, yet had not passed it ere he saw, crouching upon the granite steps, the idiot heir to all that show and wealth. Harvard had heard of this unfortunate being, but had never seen him before He went back a few feet, to catch another look at the poor creature, who, as if amazed and outraged at the intrusion, leaped over the steps, and stood howling, or savagely jumping nearer, in a truly frightful manner.

" Don't distress yourself; I am sure no one would wish to look at you very long," thought Harvard, ready to move on, when the idiot's keeper, accompanied by a tall, elegantly-dressed gentleman of disagreeable countenance, came out of the front hall. The latter angrily demanded, —

" What are you loitering here for? Don't you know that I could prosecute you? How would you like to be sent to jail? How do I know but you meant to rob,— may be set fire ? "

" Excuse me, sir. I did not mean anything wrong by stopping."

" That's your word for it. Go along. Stop! what's your name ? "

" Harvard Hoyt, sir."

" Don't *sir* me, with the air of your betters. So your name is Hoyt. Humph! Who is your father ? "

" Mr. Warren Hoyt."

" My young master is growing impatient.

May I take him in now, Mr. Torrey?" asked the keeper.

The unfortunate father gave a quick, disgusted look at this poor remnant of a large family of children, and then, as if half afraid to meet the contrast, slowly turned his eyes upon Harvard, who stood just where he had spoken, intelligent, active, full of kindness and sympathy.

"Boy, why don't you pass on? Or do you think your appearance worthy of longer notice?" demanded Mr. Torrey, when he had grown weary with gazing upon the superior of the two children. "If you do, you are mistaken. I seldom see a more ill-favored boy,— so small, sallow, thin, and old-looking; quite a fright, clothes and all! My son is sick; that's why he undoubtedly strikes you as different from the common run of children. Master Torrey does not need nor notice your pity. So you are the son of Mr. Warren Hoyt! A fine man, — a father to be proud of, boy! Ah, you've found that out!"

And in this way did Mr. Torrey revenge himself on Harvard for showing — and how innocently! — the inferiority of his son, — a revenge that only the meanest, smallest mind would have resorted to.

Harvard was too much astounded to command himself at once. At last he walked on, but glanced back ere he had wholly left the sidewalk bordering the Torrey grounds, and beheld the stricken father laboring up the long flight of granite steps with his idiot child in his arms. Harvard stifled all anger at the sight, and thought, —

"Now I see why Jimmy was treated so the other day; Mr. Torrey could not bear the looks of the bright little fellow, because his son is so unfortunate. That man deserves pity. Ah, but how could he speak so about father, whom

15

he wronged? He can not be a good man yet. Nobody can be good who speaks so."

Harvard hurried along, more thoughtful than when he left home. He had nearly reached a business street in which he wished to try his luck, when he saw a boy of about his own age crying bitterly, and alternately running and walking.

"Why, Leo Lyle! what is the matter?" asked Harvard.

"I would tell only you, for you will pity without scorning me. But look at my forehead. Do you see that great red mark?" sobbed forth Leo, lifting his hair, and showing just above the temple a long, deep cut.

"Oh, how dreadful it looks, Leo!"

"And do you see these cuts on my arms and neck?" continued Leo, exposing other wounds.

"I do. But do cover 'em up! I hate to look at them. How did you get such dreadful cuts?"

" My father gave them all to me this morning. He is a man who will give me a stone if I ask him for bread."

" Don't, Leo! "

" I will! I must! I almost hate him! You know that I am willing to do everything I can to help my parents along."

" That's the truth, Leo! "

" But this morning father was — you know what. I hate to speak the word. He called me a lazy fellow, and attacked poor mother with bad language. She had not said one unpleasant word to him, and silenced me when I undertook to speak in her defense. But I *would* defend her when he raised the carving-knife to strike her. These marks are what I got to pay for it. I am not crying for myself; it's only for her. Father's asleep now. I can't bear to leave mother with him. She is not well. I am going to get Mrs. Humphrey to stay with her to-day."

So far Leo had spoken in a low, excited tone.
Suddenly dropping his voice, he asked in a
husky, heart-full whisper, —

" Harvy, do you feel very badly when you
think Lina is dead ? "

A sudden gush of tears was all the answer
he received.   Leo continued, with impassioned
earnestness,—

" You ought not ; you must not.   She is better off than our mothers, Harry.   That is the
solemn, blessed truth. Listen, Harry. If J
could see my mother — and, oh, how I love
her ! — if I could see her at rest, I should be
glad.   I don't know what would become of me
then ; it wouldn't matter much, as long as I
knew she was in heaven."   Then, after a pause
broken by sobs, again loud and excited, Leo
cried. —

" Oh, Harvy, will the time never come when
rum shall no more be sold ? "

" I don't know," replied Harvy, very much

like one groping in pain and darkness. A moment after, radiant and hopeful, he added, —

"We — you and I, Leo — will be men some day."

"And then we can act, Harvy, — we can act!"

With this the boys clasped hands, and stood radiant with enthusiastic longings to leap the bounds that kept them from that future wherein lay the arena on which they were to be tested.

Ah, let no one say these boys are overdrawn pictures, — are unnaturally mature in thought and deed! The saddest of all truthfulness would deny such a statement. The child of the drunkard is usually a crushed or forced blossom.

Harvy's efforts at business-hunting among lawyers were put down at once by his friendlessness, youth, and small stature; although many to whom he made application favored him with lengthened glances which he might have taken as complimentary, had he been older, and given to vanity. Indeed, his fine intelligent eyes and intellectual face were often admired, as were also his respectful manners and good conduct.

He was no more successful among counting-rooms.

" We do not want a boy ; if we did, you are not large nor old enough for us," was the substance of every reply.

" What shall I do if the shoemaker thinks so ? " thought Harvy, still undaunted, still willing to push on to the worst.

He was unsuccessful in his hopes regarding a situation in a printing-office. He tried every one in the city, and, among them all, managed to dispose of his pea-nuts, engage a place as carrier for Jimmy, — and be reminded often of his small size. Yet one editor, a genius, by the way, fat, funny, and happy, proprietor of a profitable and venerable paper, gave him a glimmer of encouragement that a boy might be wanted the next year, if business increased. This was little enough hope, yet Harvard laid it up, looking with longing eyes at the library and luxurious appointments of the sanctum, and even dared to fancy himself as agreeably situated some day among the many in the dim future. Putting from his mind this acme of his glowing fancies, he repaired to the less attractive precincts of the strange individual who framed a wish in print for that incumbrance, — a boy.

This spot was not so repulsive as he had feared. The exterior of the store presented a neat and respectable appearance. The interior was quite as winning. The front shop was destitute of any individual to whom Harvard could make known the object of his call. But his timid rap upon the well-dusted counter was promptly answered by the proprietor, a highly respectable and sensible man, whose pleasant, open face and neat dress instantly prepossessed Harvard, who was invited to pass into the back shop and take a seat. The workmen appeared as respectable as their employer. This gentleman's name was Lombard, and his quick eye saw good things in Harvard. Harvard and Mr. Lombard sat a little apart, that they might talk without disturbing or being disturbed by the other occupants of the apartment. A superannuated soldier, who was reading aloud the Life of Pascal, was listened to by an appreciative audience very gratifying and striking to Harvard, whose eye brightened while he thought, — "In this place I shall not lose!"

After some conversation, Mr. Lombard was so well pleased with Harvard that he desired to engage him at once. Harvard paused a few moments before replying. Meanwhile a beggar-boy entered the store. Mr. Lombard instantly went to him, and, fancying himself unseen, gave the little mendicant a pair of good shoes.

This act decided our hero, whose best feelings were touched by such ready and delicate sympathy. Mr. Lombard invited him to dine. This invitation was accepted, for Harvard wished to see as much as possible of his master before he returned to his mother to tell her of his engagement. His eyes sparkled when serving up his innocent gossip.

"I like them all, mother. Such happy, merry beings you never saw. A nice table that looked just right, serving and all. Such a well-informed set, too! A valuable collection of books, if I am a judge, a fine piano, — the whole family play, mother. The young ladies teach, one music, the other French, in the high school. Why, Mr. Lombard is quite rich, at least we should call it rich *now*," — there listener and speaker sighed, — "and lives in good style. I like the workmen, and mean to get along well with them. Besides, that good old

soldier's reading makes the shop quite a lite-
rary retreat, I tell you."

Thus hopefully and cheerfully chatted our
hero on the eve of his apprenticeship. With
an exchange of prayerful supplication for each
other's happiness, and of tender kisses, the mother and son parted for the night, the one to
revel in golden dreams, his young spirit striving to free itself from the bonds injustice had
woven around it, the other to fear amid her
hopes and prayers.

O mothers, mothers, ye whose heartstrings
have been grasped by the torturing hands of
intemperance, ye can feel for her! None others can. God be thanked for it!

These are not dispensations of his sending, —
well for the soul that all its intuitions teach
that! But they who do send them, — how is it
with them? How will it be with them?

O mothers, whose eyes perchance have reached
this page, can you forget the time when your

first-born, feeble, puny, a child in nothing save
years, grave-faced and heavy with experience
that had notched each one of those years into
his soul as if with the sure stroke of the brand-
ing-iron, went forth from your presence with
the noble purpose to restore to you and yours
rights that wrong had taken? You must.
Maternity is not forgetful. Go back to that
day, then; and, with its memories nerving you
to action, strive with your more prosperous sisters until the greatest evil that humanity can
know is crushed beneath your feet!

You can do this. Your children are as
potter's clay in your hands.

" My son learn a shoemaker's trade! Why,
Mrs. Hoyt, I am ashamed of you. But it is
only another proof of the world's cruelty to
me. I expected something different from you,
wife," whimpered Mr. Hoyt, when informed of
Harvard's engagement.

" What had you rather he'd do, Warren ? "

" Nothing. Yet, if you think it necessary for him to do anything, — and why should it be ? — let him be a merchant's clerk," replied Mr. Hoyt, with an absurdly grand wave of his white hand.

" He tried for such a situation, and for others more agreeable to our feelings, Warren, but could obtain none."

" What! my son — Warren Hoyt's son — refused a beggarly situation when he condescended to apply for one! This statement passes my belief. Mrs. Hoyt, you must be playing upon my credulity."

" I am not, Warren."

And, in truth, her whole bearing showed that the time for pleasantry had passed.

" Father, be assured that I will not disgrace you," said Harvard, anxious to relieve his mother.

" But shoemaking is so low," said this semblance of a man, taking the larger share of the scant breakfast.

"You would not think so, father, if you could see Mr. Lombard. I will tell you all about him."

"Excuse me from hearing it. I shall not enter his presence, nor permit him to enter mine," replied Mr. Hoyt, with ludicrous hauteur.

"Jimmy, be faithful to your employers; neglect no good chance for helping mother along; attend school as regularly as possible, and study all that you can. But I needn't say this to you, for you have always been the best boy in the world," was the substance of Harvard's parting injunction to his brother, who, amid sobs, answered vehemently, —

"Yes, and I'll try to be just like you!"

Harvard clasped the little fellow to his heart, in a gush of mingled sorrow and affection.

"Girls!" he continued, mastering his feelings, " be gentle, obedient, kind to mother, and," stooping to whisper in their ears, " patient with poor father."

" We will," they answered, clinging around his neck.

" I think," cried Grace, " if you'll only give me your thimble and needles I can help mother a great deal more. Mine don't seem to move as fast as yours, brother."

" You shall have them," said Harvard.

Harvard turned toward his mother with filling eyes and throbbing heart. As he looked at her thin frame and care-worn face, he saw how much there was for him to do.

"Blessings on you, my boy!" was all her lips could utter, though next they were pressed upon his forehead in an agony of feeling too deep for expression.

" I am going, father. It is the best thing I can do now. But by and by I hope I shall be able to do much better for all hands. You don't feel very badly about my being a shoemaker, father?"

Ah, Harvard's heart yearned toward his erring parent!

"Harvard, you'll oblige me by not speaking to nor expecting notice from me in the street. Never before did a Hoyt degrade himself to the level of a shoemaker," replied Mr. Hoyt, haughtily withdrawing from the group gathered around Harvard.

The younger children looked after him in amazement, scarcely believing their own ears. Jimmy breathed very hard and loud, while his chubby fists doubled up of themselves.

Harvard looked at his mother for consolation for the outraged feelings this harsh speech awoke, and thought, while seizing and pressing her dear hand for comfort, "If she can suffer in silence, can not I?"

And then he went forth into the broad world to seek his fortune, and to retrieve the fallen ones he left behind.

CHAPTER XIV.

" The blue of heaven is larger than the cloud."

ARVARD found his new companions more
or less intelligent; none of them gradu-
ates from the highest public schools of
the city, but steady, of good principles, and cul-
tivated manners. They felt interested in the
grave little fellow, who evidently suffered much
from various causes, though as evidently resolved to master his trade, and reflect credit
upon it. Many a dress, toy, orange, or pair of
shoes did the kind fellows send home by Harvard, who at such times could only thank them
by glistening eyes, where quick tears stood from
gratitude and happy anticipations. He did not
attend the evening school, for the same kind

240

fellows offered to help him on in his studies,
and did, to his and their satisfaction. He sed-
ulously attended Sabbath school and church,
as when at his dear mother's home. With a
delicate tact Mr. Lombard paid the lad's salary
weekly. And this sum, with the pay for odd
jobs at cobbling which Harvard was encouraged
to do by the whole shop, added to what Marion,
James, and the girls earned, a long time formed
the entire maintenance of the Hoyt family.
Odd moments Harvard ever employed in reading and study, which he must do, he reasoned,
if his aspirations were to be realized. Then,
animated by the kindness he received, his own
spirit grew to be more and more that of the
missionary, moving him to be thoughtful of less
fortunate boys. He liked to pass as much of
his spare time as possible with his mother at
her workstand, — she hearing his lessons, aid-
ing him in learning them, or listening to his
reading or conversation. He knew his poor

16

father had been liberally educated, and, for the purpose of enticing him to his fireside, tried to gain a knowledge of history, and of the leading and important events of the times. He had often tried to become the pupil of his father, who would never be induced to tax his time and patience so far. .Sometimes Mr. Hoyt was surprised into prolonged conversations with his son; sometimes he invited them, to his own astonishment. But the latter usually happened when he was too weary or shabby to go out, or had been " snubbed " by *bon vivants* into temporary disappearance from the public.

Mr. Lombard was occasionally present at these times, and aided Harvy in his filial efforts to reform his father. He invited him to attend church with him, and also to join a temperance organization of which he was a member. But Mr. Hoyt always refused, and could not forget that Mr. Lombard was an artisan; but, somehow, he never forgot to treat him politely, if haughtily.

Harvard in the mean time taught his sensitive heart to feel less pain at the oft-denied recognition of his father when they accidentally met on the street.

Indeed, Mr. Hoyt sometimes debated in his own mind whether or not it was his duty to notice a shoemaker at all, even if it were his son. Yet he did not hesitate to live beneath the roof provided by that son's income; nor did he scruple to wear boots and shoes made by those industrious young hands; nor did he blush to smoke and drink — whenever he could steal a chance — upon the hard earnings of the boy so ingloriously ignored.

When Harvard had been at his trade a year, his sunbeam flashed brightly upon him. Aurora was in high health, and dressed in beautiful attire Her bright face quite dazzled our hero, who was required by Mr. Lombard to learn the object of her visit.

" I have come to get four pairs of toilet slippers made, — presents for friends," explained the sweet voice, that also said in gay accents, —

" Why, I meet you when I least expect to! "

Harvard smiled, and asked after the health of " Miss Horne," who he learned was quite well.

When the slippers were finished, it was his duty to hand them to Aurora.

" Oh, they are made beautifully! " she said, when, like one competent to do so, she had examined them thoroughly.

" I suppose you don't care to inquire after the health of Miss Horne to-day? " she asked quizzically. .

" I do, indeed. How is she? "

" Very well. And what else? Guess."

" I can not. Please tell me."

" She is going to marry our Peter! "

" Is he worthy of her ? " asked Harvard.

" I suppose so. We like him," replied Aurora.

" Then I am glad for her. She deserves a great deal of happiness," said Harvard.

" You are so different from other boys! Fred Uhland is more cruel and foolishly grand, and a greater dunce than ever. Uncle George Umber has returned from Germany ; he is looking like an ape, as any of Mr. Torrey's pupils may be expected to."

" Both may make good men, however."

" I don't see how. Never mind them now. The other day I found out, by listening to my parents' talk, that you and I are distantly related. Did you know it, Harvard ? "

" Yes."

" Why did you not tell me ? "

" I dared not. You are rich, and I am poor."

" That's nothing to keep us apart."

With these impulsive words, Aurora extended her hand to Harvard, which he grasped in both his.

They stood thus a moment, gazing into each other's eyes, and then, with hasty promises of mutual remembrance, they separated.

" You know that lovely little girl, then ? " observed Mr. Lombard when Harvard returned to his seat.

" Yes, sir," simply replied the lad.

" Know her ? To be sure he does. Isn't she some sort of a cousin to him ? " observed the old soldier, who was " acquainted with the pedigree of the entire human family," — so the workmen declared.

" I did not know it," said Mr. Lombard.

" Well, it is so. And so are many of our richest and most influential people relatives of his," continued the old soldier, full of his favorite theme.

" But never mind, my boy," he suddenly added, upon rather tardily witnessing the distress he had caused,—"never mind; you'll beat 'em all. It is in you; I can see that. 'It is good for a man that he bear the yoke in his youth.' You are trained to self-reliance, and will brave the tempest that crushes those who are not. Only keep on the right track; be always temperate, faithful, industrious, God-loving and God-fearing, and you will succeed in any path you choose. You'll be all that, my boy; your speech and actions show you have taken the Bible for your guide."

"I hope Harvard won't forget us when he is the great man you predict," said one of the workmen, pleasantly.

Harvard declared he never could, even if he did become great, which he did not expect.

One morning he made a confession to Mr. Lombard, which did not seem to surprise that excellent man, who, after a few moments' thought, observed,—

"Do you know anything of it? Latin is something worth studying, I think."

"Your eldest daughter and two of these kind fellows here," pointing to a couple of fine-looking young men, "have helped me on some distance," replied Harvard.

"And you want to go through to the end of it, and everything else, if you have a chance?" quizzed Mr. Lombard.

"I should, indeed," replied Harvard.

"Well, I think Parker Jewell will help you in Latin. He has a heart and head large enough for a dozen men. I have an errand down that way; I might just as well do it now," said Mr. Lombard, removing his leather apron, and preparing for the walk, which, ten minutes before, he had not thought of taking.

Labor, patience, study, courage, and hope made a memorable year for Harvard. Mr. Jewell was a faithful teacher and friend. Nor is this all that rendered the year a golden one.

Mrs. Hoyt improved in health and spirits, and bade fair to enjoy both, would fortune but continue kind.

And this is the last year of Harvard's apprenticeship. The three years had been pleasant and profitable.

" What has become of your old wish to learn printing, my son ? " asked Marion, when Harvard had been for some months one of Mr. Lombard's journeymen, and lived with her in a very comfortable home.

" Lost sight of in better plans," he smilingly replied, looking up from the volume in hand. " I intend, mother, to study law. I can do it, and yet, with Jimmy's help, keep as good a home as this," he slowly and thoughtfully added.

" Margie and I can help more than we have done. We are becoming quite expert with the needle, ' said Grace.

"But you must not neglect your books," replied Harvard.

"There is no danger of that, with such a brother," merrily said Margie.

"You have set a shining example to all of us, my son," said Marion, with affection and pride.

Harvard disclaimed this, and, with his old habit of blushing, proceeded : —

"When I have mastered law, the endless West will give me a chance to practice my profession."

"You won't leave us!" cried the girls.

"No. We will all go. We shall each find enough to do there."

"I shall be a leather-merchant," said James, now an apprentice to Mr. Lombard, and an inmate of that gentleman's family, in place of his brother, whose praise was on many tongues. "And, mother," continued James, "when we are rich enough we will buy back Auburndale."

Then, lowering his voice, he added, in an indistinguishable whisper, " When we do that, mother, I do believe that poor father will be as good as — as anybody."

The mother kissed the broad, open brow of this ambitious boy, and hoped his wild dream would be realized; at any rate, she hoped prosperity might be granted him, so that his young heart might no more feel the cruel pressure of want and disappointment; or, if for further discipline those olden troubles must continue, that they would be permitted to bring faith and resignation. Many a streak of silver banded the head of Marion, and many a grief had left deep traces on the face once so smooth and fair; but seldom had she been so happy as at this moment, when her children, true, loving, respected, were gathered in health and joyous anticipation around her. Truly, God, through all, had liberally blessed her.

" I am glad that Mr. Jewell continues to take

an interest in and be patient with father," said
Grace, who had great faith in the clergy. "I
think he will help him become a better man.
Harvard, how intelligently father talked with
you and Mr. Jewell last evening! He quite
charmed me."

"Your father is a fine scholar; few surpass
him," said Marion, with a sigh.

"Oh, mother, never sigh! He'll come out
right yet!" cried Jimmy, who had taken supper with the family.

As if to augment the general joy, Warren
returned home sober and peaceable.

He had taken tea, he said, with Mr. Lombard,
— how Harvard opened his eyes! — and really
he seemed a prime sort of a man, and had a
stylish home, and very handsome family, especially the young ladies, who were equal in
every respect to any he had ever met, not even
excepting Marion in her palmiest days: this
was said in a playful tone. He really had no

idea of it; he was astonished to find so much cultivation and refinement among the working classes. He thought he should like to see more of Mr. Lombard, and he rather wished he had made his acquaintance sooner. Perhaps, after all, it had not been so bad for Harvard to learn the trade. He intended to visit the shop some day.

How Harvard blessed Mr. Lombard for noticing his father, despite his opposition and disdain!

But Mr. Lombard had a living desire to help the poor and needy and unfortunate. Often trying, never until that day had he found Mr. Hoyt willing to notice him.

Under God, he had restored to many a man lost honor and confidence. And his efforts were made with so much delicacy and tact that those favored seldom saw how much they were indebted to him.

CHAPTER XV.

"WHO WOULD HAVE THOUGHT IT?"

"Then let us pray that come it may,
As come it will for a' that,
That sense and worth, o'er all the earth,
May bear the gree and a' that."

AURORA, child, you are seventeen, and, as nearly as your parents can judge, destitute of proper pride."

"I can't help it, mother."

"But you don't try to. And you ought, for not many families can boast of such descent. A half-dozen consecutive generations of our family have been the aristocracy of the country," continued Mrs. White, in a reproachful tone.

"So I have heard from infancy, mother."

254

"Then think soberly of what you are," implored Mrs. White.

"Born of the dust; doomed to eternal woe unless I accept pardon purchased on the cross; and, when my span is ended, to have my poor body laid low in the dust for worms to feed upon. That is what I am, mother," replied Aurora, with touching gravity and a dreamy manner.

"Ugh! What horrible ideas! Where you learned them is more than I can imagine. Again I command you to think what you are."

"Hadn't I better think what I may become?" asked the girl, her lip quivering with the exquisite tenderness of her sensibilities.

"If I have any claim upon your affection, child, never employ that manner and language again," said Mrs. White in a low tone, plucking nervously at her rich dress.

"Forgive me, mother; I did not mean to wound you. But life is so crowded with sad as well as glad lessons, that I can not always lose sight of the former in my enjoyment of the latter."

" But the sad lessons are not for you.   They come not near you."

" I don't know, mother.   I sometimes think they do."

" Give me an instance, please."   And Mrs. White smiled securely.

" You saw the young man, my bow to whom gave rise to this conversation ? "

" Yes.   Go on, child."

" He, mother — "

" Why do you pause, Aurora ? "

" Because I'm afraid that what I have to say will give you pain."

" I am not concerned.   Go on, Aurora," replied Mrs. White, looking curiously and jealously into her daughter's face.

" He, mother, is the son of your cousin, Marion Hoyt."

" How came you to discover that ? "

" Through the unkindness of my grandmother. I hate to remember aught against her, but you have not forgotten when his father broke into her dinner-party ? "

" Proceed."

" On that occasion, in Sally's kitchen, I saw him first, mother. But I did not learn the facts then, — not until recently. Sally was my informant, and a most unwilling one. But the curiosity started so long ago, lightened by a little gossip that reached me the other day, would be repressed no longer."

" What was the gossip ? "

" That, by what would almost seem to be superhuman efforts, he was getting a fine education. Our minister's wife was so informed by Mrs. Jewell. She told me the story, and also gave me quite an insight into the past and present condition of the Hoyt family."

" Truly ' our minister's wife ' might have

17

been better employed than in scandalizing my feelings so. Of course she knew Marion to bo my cousin."

" She did not assume to," gently replied Aurora.

" But she did know, you may depend upon it. I detect her making unpleasant comments concerning the matter, and will sit under her husband's preaching no longer. As it is, I am weary of him ; he is not the smartest Unitarian minister the world has ever known, and has always been too friendly with ministers of other denominations ! "

" Don't be angry with him, mother, just because his good wife innocently, in speaking of the frequency of poor young people rising to eminence, happened to cite Harvard Hoyt as a youth destined to make a stir in the world."

" Don't dictate," replied Mrs. White, looking a little ashamed. " If the boy was sent to the kitchen by my mother, it was the proper place for him. Though, no doubt, he was set on by his mother, who very likely had a hope that we would reinstate her at Auburndale, and endow her with means to lead an idle, extravagant life."

" I can not think she would desire to live in that way, if she ever did."

"I think I know her better than you do. Perhaps she thought we would offer to adopt him at once."

" I do not imagine that she had any such idlo fancy, mother."

" But it did not follow that you must keep up the boy's acquaintance."

" I suppose not, mamma," she answered mischievously, " but I have met him many times since."

" Aurora, I always said you lacked proper pride. I shouldn't wonder if you had called upon his mother."

"No ; I met him once on the street, and

once in the shop where he was learning his trade."

"Remember, you are not to notice him any more. Let's see,—he's rather under nineteen. There he is again. What homespun clothes! He hasn't even the pride of other young mechanics. They will wear clothes as good as the best, usually. You needn't notice him this time. Let us cross to the other side of the street, Aurora."

"In all the mud?"

"Yes, anything rather than have you recognize him again. I wish we had not come out shopping this morning, or had not left our carriage so far down street. But it is tiresome to keep entering and leaving it, while the stores are so numerous."

"Mother, I do not wish to inconvenience you; so I will not speak to Harvard this time," said Aurora.

Harvard read the proud lady's desire in the

withering glance she gave him. But he bent his gaze for a single moment on Aurora, who read in it his perfect understanding of affairs.

" Where do you suppose I have been this morning, Mrs. White ? " asked Mr. White at dinner that day.

" I can not guess," replied Mrs. White.

" Have you any curiosity ? "

" A trifle. Where ? "

" To Willowglen. It's not the place it was. Bats and rats make their home there. The willows form as splendid a shade as ever ; but to one standing outside the place has a desolate look, and it seems like gazing through into a pathless forest. I went down the avenue, now grass-grown and neglected, and entered the mansion. Every hinge was rusty and creaky, and every room moldy and dilapidated. No, Willowglen is a different place from what it was."

" Willowglen ? Who lives there, father ? "

"Nobody. It once belonged to the Mayburns, relatives of your mother."

"The paternal home of Mrs. Hoyt, father?"

"Hum! Yes."

"What a pity such changes take place, father!"

"Sometimes it happens so, child. But, Mrs. White, whom do you suppose I found there, taking on terribly?"

"I can not guess, I'm sure."

"Mrs. Hoyt."

"How in the world did she get there?"

"Walked, most likely. She was curious to see it once more, the same as I was. The present owner is a childless widower, now in Europe. It has passed through many hands since I had a claim upon it."

"Did you speak to the woman, husband?"

"No. I would have spoken, but she looked at me in a way that seemed to declare she wanted no notice from me. She was always confoundedly distant and haughty when she pleased, wife."

"Once she could be. But now,—pride and poverty are apt to go together, though," replied Mrs. White.

Aurora left the table in tears. Then her parents talked in a low tone for some minutes. Soon after Harvard read in the public journals the departure of the Whites for Europe. He would have liked to travel. But because he could not, and others could, did not give him a single regret, nor move him from his usual course a moment. He worked hard all day, studied far into the night, and continued to be the light of his home. The star of his youthful hopes still beckoned him on and upward,— he indeed aspired high.

Aurora was placed at a Parisian finishing-school, quite against her democratic predilections for American educational institutions. In three years, to her intense joy, she was de-

clared " finished." About this period, her uncle,
George Umber, once Mr. Torrey's pupil, filled
a drunkard's grave. Though young when he
died, he had established for himself so unfortunate a reputation that no respectable persons
would admit him to their house. Frederic
Uhland was pursuing the same career. Mrs.
Umber did not long survive her disgrace.
Upon her decease, almost the first movement
of her husband was in the direction of the
residence of the Hoyts, where he was always
made welcome. For this privilege he made them
many timely presents. He seemed to know
just when the rent was due, and never failed
to send fuel the very day it was wanted. Ere
he died, he had sought and found pardon at the
foot of the cross. He left to his " beloved
cousin, Marion Hoyt, the sum of one thousand
dollars, and to each of her children five hundred." Mrs. Uhland desired to contest his will,
feeling unwilling to see Marion in better cir-

cumstances, and envious of Harvard, who she prophesied would be nothing, after all the stir he had made, or the stir people had made about him.

But her declarations against the sanity of her father were set aside by competent judges. Mrs. White, though still absent from home, also sent her protest against permitting Marion to enjoy one cent of money by " that strange will."

" I would make no trouble over so small a legacy, mother," advised Aurora, who would have said the same had the sum been much larger. " One of these days, the Hoyt family will be deemed, even by yourself, to be worthy the notice of the highest in the land."

" How absurd, child ! "

" Not at all, mother; see if my words fall short of the truth ; " and Aurora looked pleased as she spoke. Mrs. White sighed, and wondered if, after all the pains taken, Aurora still lacked " proper pride."

The Whites remained abroad until Aurora had completed her twenty-seventh year. No persuasions of her parents could induce her to marry. Her rare traits of character could not be overlooked, and many friends with aching hearts saw her embark for her native land.

"Home at last!" she murmured, as the grounds of Auburndale, in the richness of their spring beauty, burst upon her view. She became again, in familiar places, or wherever duty called her, a friend to the needy and sorrowing; not that while abroad she had been the reverse, for many an empty purse had she filled, many a wounded heart had she soothed, and many a kind word and pitying tear had she dropped, during her sojourn among strangers. She took a class in Sabbath school, much to her parents' horror, and shocked them more by presently connecting herself with the evangelical church to which that Sabbath school belonged. Then, more than ever, did the beau-

ties of her character develop, and even to the
tender admiration of her worldly parents, for
whose conversion she constantly prayed, and
who at length seemed to be nearing her God.

The winter following his return, Mr. White
took his family westward.

"We may expect something grand to-morrow," said a gentleman at dinner, the day succeeding the establishment of the White family
at the best hotel in a large city.

"Yes; of higher order than we usually get,
though I think our western lawyers are in no
wise inferior. This one is keen, subtle, thor-
oughly-read, humane, and just. He can not be
bribed to deal wickedly. He might have been
independently rich, young as he is, would he
but have silenced his conscience for hire. But
no! he is that excellent being, — a Christian
lawyer. Would there were more like him!"

"I echo all that most heartily," replied the

first speaker. Aurora was so near she could not avoid hearing the conversation.

"Self-made, too," continued the first speaker.

"Almost always the best," rejoined the other.

"The name of this lawyer?" politely asked Mr. White, intending to make the acquaintance of one so lauded.

"Hoyt. He was born in Massachusetts; saw hard times there; struggled through everything, sir! He will get the case, — one of right (poor enough clients, sir!) against might (which happens to be rich, sir); but he'll gain the day!" replied one of the gentlemen, with unction.

Mr. and Mrs. White exchanged glances, both thinking, "Who would have thought it?" Aurora looked at the gentleman with interest, while her father asked questions enough of him to have tried his patience and courtesy, had the subject been less interesting.

Mrs. White and Aurora were among the

most noticed ladies adorning the gallery of the
court-house next day. At length the hero
entered the arena. Could it be he, so tall
and grand? His remarkable beauty of face
and mien astonished Aurora. His deep, rich
voice impressed upon every mind golden truths
in the language of genius. Ah! even the
haughty Mrs. White was aroused. Miser-like,
Aurora hung upon his words, weighed every
point, criticised each outburst of passionate
eloquence. Suddenly his towering form vi-
brated; his voice trembled; his words grew
less clear; his deep eyes looked, and looked
again.

He could not mistake that face. It was Aurora, the friend of his childhood, whom he so
unexpectedly beheld! Ah! how glad was he
to be able to meet her thus,—to show her that
her friendship had not been misplaced!

He regained composure, and continued, growing more and more eloquent.

When he had ended, "A triumph! A signal triumph!" was on every tongue, while thunders of applause shook the house.

One radiant glance, half shy, half seeking his, was ample reward for Harvard.

Mrs. White immediately busied herself in telling ladies about her that the brilliant young lawyer was her cousin. At this Aurora dropped her head.

"Mrs. White, we must have our magnificent young cousin here often," said Mr. White, as he entered her room late the next morning.

"Certainly, husband."

"I have just returned from a supper given in honor of him, — a right royal one, too. All the lights of the city were present to do him honor. He is still single. At the close of his plea, I was among the first to offer my congratulations. I took his arm, and walked down street with him. He says his family is doing well. His father is in lucrative business; his sisters are teaching; his brother, a prosperous shoe and leather dealer, and married to the youngest Miss Lombard; and our old friend Marion is in excellent health and spirits."

" All of which is good news, husband."

" Wife, he dines with us to-day."

" Nothing could give me greater pleasure Who would have thought it, though!"

Aurora, standing before her mirror, swept her sunny hair over her face, ashamed of her parentage.

" Wife," continued Mr. White, " by the way, he is the most zealous hater of exhilarating drink that I ever met. Not a drop touched his lips. And, 'pon honor, wife, his example was contagious!"

Here, simply mentioning his marriage with Aurora, we leave Harvard Hoyt, feeling the while a tender regret, as one does when the smiling face of a dear friend is lost to our straining view.

Child of sorrow, is yours a harder lot than that which, through God, disciplined and perfected Harvard's character?

Some weary little heart, with tattered robe and aching limbs, and sigh that Jesus listens to, may whisper " yes."

To all such, and to those in whose life-cup there is any mingling of gall, and to those whose days begin and end in sunshine, we answer, Strive for the right. Do not despair. It is our privilege, nay, more, our duty, to strive for the right.

Do not despair; you will conquer. Buckle on the armor of patience, perseverance, hope, grace, " charity that suffereth long and is kind," and at each successive step your path will be less thorny, your sky less troubled, your purpose nearer fulfillment, your salvation closer at hand.

THE END.